Introduction

My interest in history, science, art and religion has always made me wonder about the origins of human civilization. Language and the written word can only tell us about ourselves, for as long as we had possessed those attributes. Beyond that, only art and science can help us to deduce what people were like before history was written. Religion is a dominant part of the human spirit, which has existed before perhaps even art. Indeed, art most likely was the expression of human kind's first awakening of self-awareness and its mortality.

Hank Wilson

Chapter 1.

The East.

When the darkening west skies became the color of wine, and the west wind blew as it rarely did, it blew with a constant pressure on the body as when riding a horse at full gallop. Fear ran through the whole of the countryside for all knew what the west wind would bring. History would repeat itself again and again, and in a matter of days the masts of the big ships would grow swiftly out of the sea, rising up by the thousands ahead of a westward storm. The people of Eastland would have a few wild and windy days and nights to prepare for the onslaught of an attack by their only foe. The monsters from the other side of The Sea would land as a storm, followed by a terrible torrent of wind, rain and waves. The killers and rapers, maimers and thieves, the burners and butchers who were the reasons most feared to live, only to live to be caught by the ones from Westland, the other side of The Sea. The spacious waters bought precious time for the Eastlanders as the west wind blew rarely. Maybe a generation would pass between blows or perhaps two. Almost long enough to forget if it was not for the stories passed down around campfires and a burned out castle left unrestored for each time the west wind blew. Burnt and broken stone foundations as if their only existence was to count, each representing the fateful morning that it succumbed to the storm. Numbering in the hundreds not a soul dared to count them, as it would be a bad thing to know what number was next. It would be the only thing any Eastlander could think about, that unknown number. Better not to know it and to think about living and loving, working and having children who would grow up to fear the Westlanders. All the campfire tales told over the years about them would spring to life in memories of death. The sky grew black as the purple clouds obscured the sun. The night was chilled and starless, and the wind blew relentlessly.

The Eastlanders Queen was too young to have experienced a storm but she had in her minds eye a first hand glimpse from her elders' tales of the few they had known. The child princess Helina would absorb the elder's campfire stories as fantastic tales to be recited for entertainment until she was seven years of age. She learned of her own mortality one night when the sagas were made more real without the caution yielded to young children. She remembered being angry, not so much at the Westlanders, but at the realization that all children face on that fateful day when one learns that someday, one must die. It did not matter the cause. She remembered that she was seven because it was her birthday. As writing did not exist in the east or the west, storytelling was what gave continuity to the lives of the peoples living by The Sea. Not much was known about the laws of the west but the worst transgression in the east was to lie. Even if murder, rape and thievery existed among the Eastlanders, lying would still be the crime of disdain. There were no courts or jails in Eastland for none were needed. On the rare occasion that a storyteller was caught embellishing tales of old, he or she would become a temporary pariah until the people forgave. It was a sad thing to be rejected by your loved ones but the rejection was usually short lived as the Eastlanders hated to not love, all the more reason for not understanding the west, and for fearing them. The west knew not love.

Queen Helina's body was a single virgin not yet twenty years of age but her intuitive insight combined with a keen and sarcastic wit would give balance to a tender heart unaffected by darker times. Those lie in the future. Her spirit was yet undamaged and her mortality she so feared as a child seemed to have receded into the closet of the mind. Things were about to change and she would be forced to unlock that closet door and confront not only the monsters from the far side of The Sea, but the monster in her mind as well.

Eastland was an idyllic place not only for the lush and varied landscape, from its crystalline white sandy beaches that gave way to a carpet of ice plants and all types of palms, to its rolling blue hills, green fields and finally the rugged cliffs and snow topped mountains with numerous caves, but also for its culture. The people were soft-spoken and generally calm. There were no distinctive facial features to make them a specific race except that everyone had the same gold-green eyes, but rather they seemed unclassifiable, in the same way that a certain color had no name but require a detailed description of it to explain it. What made them a collective were their mannerisms and attitudes. Even the children gently strolled and moved with deliberateness like actors on a stage. Just as there were no laws, there were no rules of manners or attitudes, for none were needed. At times they seemed of one mind and all the people knew when it would be time for certain chores such as the annual harvesting of different wild plants and fruits. They were in tuned to the season's every nuances. The prevailing south wind would change for a month out of the year and bring down from the North Mountains, the sweet smell of the edible flowers that could be harvested, dried and eaten the rest of the year. They were not agrarian nor did they practice animal husbandry. The animals were mostly wild yet as passive as the people. They didn't fear the people for hunting didn't exist either. They were not eaters of meat or fish. They planted no crops and chopped no trees. They walked softly on their beloved land. They had no boats accept for driftwood that was used for play on the waters of The Sea. Twice a year the men and the boys would venture through the East Mountain's pass and beyond the great waterfall that fed the cold stream, which ended its journey in a lagoon by the beach. The jungle trail through the pass would give way to the high forests of the plateau with no name. Nobody knew what lie beyond the forest as after a time it would become so thick with connivers and Maples that not even the deer could penetrate. No stranger had ever come out of the forest so for the Eastlanders, it was the end of the earth, beyond only blackness. The journey east was a time of gathering of mushrooms and maple for the men and boys but the pilgrimage had a deeper meaning. It was a month of separation from the women and the girls, not an escape but a time of learning for the children. Men would teach the boys the gentle art of courting the girls, the ways of walking softly on the earth, and how to survive a great storm from the Westlanders as well as the great atmospheric storms that would bring them. The number one rule was to hurt no one. The second rule was to survive. During the separation the women would train the girls on the art of seduction without submission. They were taught that it is the longing for another that is more pleasurable than the having. This tension filled strategy was the hallmark of the Eastlanders as it would develop the strengths of hope and love that had helped them to survive the uncounted storms from the west over the millennia. The girls were also taught how to avoid being raped or captured by the Westlanders. "Run!" Eastlanders were exceptional runners for this very reason, and the women and the girls were not only fast runners but could zig and zag and hop like a wild animal was being pursued as prey. It was survival and it would harm no one. There would be no separation now. The west wind had changed all that. Now was a time for preparing for the coming storm and for all the peoples of Eastland to meet with the Queen and the Elders to discuss survival strategies. Only the elders knew the fear of the storm for they had survived one, and a few of them had survived two. The people and even the Queen would turn to them now for their fears were only imagined as the elders' fears were memories.

Since there were no laws in Eastland the Queen had no power. That word had no meaning in this society. The only definition that the east had for the word power was "west", for they equated power with evil. They knew the word evil as well and it also meant "west". The west had every connotation of darkness and suffering attached to it. Since the storms were so infrequent, most never knew evil but they were aware that it existed. Evil was almost an abstract term with a face and a direction. Evil was far removed such as death is to a child's thinking. Evil was approaching fast, perhaps by morning or three days at most, and the people of Eastland with their collectiveness knew the urgency and they instinctively knew what to do. Meet at the castle to receive instruction and advice from the source of history, the elder storytellers and the beloved virgin queen. The castle itself was not large and formidable; there was no reason for a fortress as all resistance to the west was useless. There was a huge courtyard ample enough to contain the entire population for just such a meeting. There would be no debate, only listening to the elders while Helina smiled on affectionately. After the listening, the Queen would issue a request of cooperation, which would be heeded without debate. "My beloved. I embrace you this hour to act. Put on your costumes of the stage and become the bold ones that you practiced to be all these years during the clear cool nights of the north wind when we all empathized with the Westlanders. We became them to try to understand their ways. We could never. But we can gain strength as a collective with our trust in each other and our love for them. When they come, and they will, they will land on our beaches as a collective. As we all know from the storytellers, they are big. They are fast moving and wear clothing of animal skins and they eat the meat from those animals raw. They drink fermented blood and as the stories have told, they eat their own children. They talk to an invisible person whom they say is all-powerful. They cut trees to build their big boats each of which will hold a thousand of them. They are coming with this wind that increases as I speak. Because their boats ride the wind they can only come here once every generation or two. We know that they use the time between the west winds to cut more trees and to build bigger boats and to make new weapons of which we can only imagine. They will come to kill us. They will come to eat our children and to rape our women. They will torture us and drink our blood and use the fat from our bodies as fuel to burn this castle as a symbol of authority. We know what we must do to help insure that our people will continue after the storm. We must bury the children deep in the caves under the earth. The elderly must dress in costume to greet them as they arrive while our young girls run for the dark forest on the unnamed plateau. Our young boys must go to the North Mountains tonight and not return until it is safe and the Westlanders have drunk their fill of our blood and once again burn the castle. They can only stay a few days for the east wind will blow for a week or so until the protective south wind returns. Be not fearful as many of us will die a terrible death, some will survive to continue the collective spirit of peace and love that we are and have always been." The west wind increased just then to where the Queen was no longer audible and the crowd dispersed without haste to do the things in preparation for the arrival of the Westlanders.

Chapter 2

The West

On the other side of The Sea, the terrain was much different from the eastern shores. No crystalline sandy beaches but slippery red mud made from where clay met the water's edge. The result was blood red surf that brought trash and carcasses of animals and humans smashing into the shore with the stench of death always present. Houses made from dried red clay bricks without roofs were jammed into every nook of the coastal plain that would give way to taller, two and three story structures with mountains of trash and bones filling every vacant space. These heaps had been walked on for a millennium or more and were indeed the roads and pathways for getting around the city. The city, a red brick structure as far as one could see to the great sand hills that delineated what appeared to be the edge of the population. As you walked up a path you would realize that the edifices were buried deep into the heaps with natural stairways that emerged from the ground where untold levels of the buildings lie beneath that heap. Smoke and the smell of cooked and rotting flesh rose from all directions until most of the city was blocked from view. The heap of a city rose up what appeared to be a hill but was virtually an inhabited garbage dump. After discovering the hidden living areas it became apparent that this was a city of hundreds of thousands or perhaps millions of wretched folk living atop each other in a tangled mass of unplanned sprawl. After the city, and over the great sand hills the huge industrial lagoon revealed its purpose at once. Thousands of colossal wooden ships were docked and being built or repaired. There was not a tree in sight nor a living dog or cat or any other life except for the countless people of Westland. No child played, nobody sang and there was not a smile to be seen. The folks were indeed large, at least a head higher than the average Eastlander. They were dirty and wore the filthy skins of animals that were not tailored in the least. Some of the clothing was a freshly killed carcass and one man wore a pig that was still alive but just barely. The workers on the ships were the most wretched of all. Tied about their necks were slender ropes that cut into their flesh when they breathed. They were long threads that dragged the ground and were attached to heavy stones which sat on wooden trap doors in the dock where the rock could in an instant be released into the greasy black water, either pulling the worker down with it, or snapping the head clean. They worked very hard and without stopping even for the shortest time to stretch a back or to have a drink.

The ships were incredibly huge in length breadth and height excluding the masts. They were built in the style of the red brick city, more like a heap of wood instead of a planned sailing vessel. Several stories stacked atop each other with windows here and there with no rhythm or style. The wood was course and splintered logs barely planed to fit and much pitch was used as a sealer. The ones in dry dock revealed the undersides as having pitch a foot thick in places in an attempt to keep the behemoths afloat. The masts are not single trees but many lashed together with crude twine. They tapered getting progressively thinner at the top and the bottom third was covered with the same black pitch. There is nothing elegant about the boats and they would hold a thousand warriors, a few thousand head of wild oxen and cattle. Fish would be caught along the way in great nets, usually on the return trip. No storage of grains or dried fruits and vegetables were taken. The Westlanders were strictly carnivorous. A thousand barrels of fermented blood were lashed to the main deck with a large pit of stones at deck's center for an eternal fire for cooking meat and heating the blood for they liked their blood body temperature or slightly warmer. The stone pits would be used for cooking the children of Eastland as tradition would dictate this affair, as well as appeasing the invisible almighty one. The west had always had the invisible one, and a storytelling tradition that evolved around him. He was an unforgiving god who controlled all aspects of the Westlanders' culture and traditions. The east had no such god. They were a collective spirit between themselves and the land, wind and water as well as all living things. In a very real sense they believed that even the people of the west was a part of them as they were living creatures as well. This contradiction of the fear of the west and their love of all things was the dichotomy at the very core of their being. The west had no such attachment for the east but held the belief that the invisible one's hatred for them was the engine, which drove the west to attack the east on every occasion that the wind allowed. The wind was the breath of their god and the command to action and the more brutal the actions the closer to god they became.

It was a mystery where the enormous amounts of timber came from for the construction of the ships, for all one could see was red clay and beyond the black lagoon only sand hills that stretched to the horizon. There were trails that snaked through the sand hills from the lagoon and if they were followed a great distance inland one could see the source of the great timbers. It was a mighty forest that once reached the sea that had been pushed back by clear cutting, requiring a three days journey on horseback to get there. The Westlanders treated their own land with a scorched earth method of cutting trees and killing every living thing in what once was a primordial and lush paradise. Then the prevailing south wind would dry out the land and leave it a barren waste of sand dunes in which a scorpion could not survive. There was no metal cutting tools for bronze had not yet been discovered and the workers used fire to burn out the roots of the big trees to weaken them after which teams of horses and men would pull them down with brute force. The fires would spread to destroy what grasses were left and finish off the entire ecosystem as the edge of the dying forest receded never to return. Nobody knew how far the forest went and nobody cared. It was an endless resource with one purpose, to build the ships to destroy the Eastlanders. There were warrior like guards on horseback who forced the labor of the entire operation by whipping and beating the slaves and horses alike. When an unfortunate man or horse died all would gather like wild dogs to eat the raw flesh and drink the blood, guards and slaves together. These were the only moments of equality for no water was available for drinking and the blood would quench the thirst of even the workhorses.

The wind had shifted from the west and there was an urgency to stop the cutting and building and the focus became making the boats ready to set sail. The sails were made of a thousand dried animal skins each and were rolled up and tied vertically to the tall masts. The biggest ships had as many as fifteen masts where the smaller boats had six or seven. Construction would continue on some unfinished boats even as the fleet of a thousand ships would set sail all loaded so heavily with food and drink and men that the waterline was many feet below the surface. The wind picked up and drove the mass of lumber and dried animal skins east as a ceremony of death would start from departure and until the return. Thousands of their own children would help to provide the nutrition for the crossing while thousands of Eastlander children would provide for the return. The invisible one would be very pleased indeed.

The wind picked up speed and blew the thousand lumbering ships out to sea. Sand that was coming from the wasted hills blasted everything and would help propel the massive fleet, boats bumping, smoke from the pits swirling ahead as the waves grew taller. Even the surf was reversed and it seemed like all of nature, all energy on the earth, the great invisible one was flowing eastward. It would take four days to make the crossing in the mighty gale but the return trip would take a month when the wind would reverse in a gentle breeze from the east, slowly turning back to the normal conditions of the prevailing south wind. If the ships did not return before the winds came around fully from the south the fleet would be pushed to the north so far that a return would be impossible. According to the old stories this had happened many times in the past two thousand years. No one knew what lie to the north for not a soul had returned from that direction. No one knew what lie to the south for the north wind never blew long enough to find anything but open sea. This was not important to the people by The Sea. The Eastlanders were happy in their land and the Westlanders' only goal was to destroy the Eastlanders.

Chapter 3

The Storm

    None of the peoples who lived on the rim of The Sea understood the size or depth of it. Since the Eastlanders never ventured out on the waters, its mysteries were deep indeed. They felt a kinship with it as they did the land and the wind and they never really questioned it any more than they questioned any other of the elements that they were a part of. To them it would be like wondering why one had a hand or a leg. They understood the beauty and the terror of the sea for they adored its variety of colors from the silvery gray color when the north wind blue to its usual aquamarine hue during the south wind. They relied on the rhythm of the surf at night to put them to sleep and the moon's reflection that were usually present during the story telling. The seam that was created where the earth, water and air met was their natural habitat. This was the place where time stood still and the zone where all of nature held its breath for eternity, until the west wind blew. Even if the Westlanders did not exist, this was the terrible part of the sea. Time no longer tarried but sped up to a pace beyond comprehension. Nature itself would exhale with a force that would grow into a howling and screaming wind to where there was no longer a seam that separated the earth, water and air. They would become one for a time and when the storm passed the seam would stitch itself neatly together again and nature's breath would be quiet as a whisper once more. It was the storms that gave such meaning to the quiet times, and the quiet times that made the storms seem all the more violent. If it were only the storms to contend with, what a paradise it would be. But the storms, the terrible storms, which brought the Westlanders, were but just an omen of the true terror in the lives of these innocent and loving folk.

The invisible one remained silent for so long that the people of West would have doubts about his existence. They believed in his return and perpetually built the ships as a reminder to his coming and out of fear of his retribution if they did not build. It was not his presence that made them the shipbuilders but his absence. It was a test of their faith to build, taking twenty or thirty years to complete a fleet that would be up to the task. Their skills as builders were inadequate hence the large numbers of vessels that were built, a good percentage would be lost on the journey but enough would survive to complete the mission. They hated the sea because it was too much like the light with its reflections and shimmering surface. They hated the sea for it was clean, and they were lovers of filth and stench. But most of all they hated the sea for its width, a protective barrier for the eastern shores.

The wind that had strengthened over the past few days had brought with it the violet gray clouds that precurse a storm. The water was slate gray and churned with rolling surf usually not present. The white caps had turned dirty and foamed and spat a salt spray that would cover the entire town at Eastland. The town was especially vulnerable to storms for it was just above the level of the water. The only true edifice was the small castle made of stone with it's short stone wall that was not for protection from anything but served only to carve out the large courtyard for meetings and such. Everyone lived in huts made from palm from and driftwood. Much of the driftwood was covered with tar, remnants of ancient boat parts that had washed ashore from the activities of the shipbuilders. Ironic that the building materials came from the source of terror when so many of the Westlanders' ships would break apart and sink either on their way to or from the destructive campaigns. The homes would not protect them from man or wind and water, nor were they meant to. Rebuilding was the price to pay for living on that seam that the Eastlanders cherished. The caves would serve them in times of storms but none chose to live in them for they were dark and damp. The ships were caught up now at the brunt of the storm as they rode the tidal wave in an eastward course which would land them directly on the beaches. What a site to see the incredible amount of logs lashed together, boats bumping and splintering on the wild waters. The smoke of the fires on board would swirl and mix with the ocean spray as men and animals fell into the drink to be caught up and crushed in the mass. The wind increased to a howl as masts snapped and animal skins were ripped and fluttering. It didn't matter then as the sails were not needed for the force of wind and water pushed everything in one direction and would increase all the while until landfall.

The once every generation storms began somewhere beyond the forests of Westland. An old legend says that the forest was so large that it would take many months to penetrate it to see what lie beyond. For this reason no one ever bothered to explore past the fringes of the thick woods of tall cedars and only went where the game led during the great hunts. Animals would be flushed out of the timbers with fire and then caught in nets and shot with bow and arrow or clubbed to death with sticks and stones. The legend also spoke of an infinitely large and hot desert of mountainous dunes and swirling winds. Passed the dunes it was said that the earth turned into a great oven of one continuous stone that spread out like the sea to the horizon. This place it was believed is where the great storms had their beginnings. This place is where the invisible one slept for twenty or thirty years at a time and when he awoke the whole earth moved and rumbled. His yawn and first breath were the stirrings, which upset the balance between the water, air and sea. Sand would always accompany the storm's first winds and the leaves would be stripped and the bark pitted by the sand blasting its way through the forest. It would gain strength as it approached the sea when an explosion of clouds would join with the forces of land and air to begin the big surge to the east. The winds would turn the ocean into great hills of water that were higher than the palms. The direction of the great storms was always the same and between the great storms there was only the occasional light rains that came out of the south which were warm, or the almost steady northern cool rains which only lasted for a month or so once a year.

Chapter 4

The General

On board the biggest of the primitive ships, at the center of the mass of lumber was General Cugat. He was a large man even for someone from the west, who towered over most of his own warriors. His head was bald with a layer of black pitch that acted as a permanent hat. His beard was long and tangled and stained with blood from eating raw flesh. His teeth were stained red and his lips were blue and chapped from the whipping sand and wind and water. He had no body hair besides the beard as Westlanders had none. He was dressed in the skin of a buck with the hair facing out to help shed water. The buck's legs covered his arms and legs and the animals' skull and antlers hanged from the back of his neck still dripping with blood. The outfit was stitched with leather up the front to his chest with only his genitalia hanging out. That was the style of a warrior and the bigger the genitalia the higher the rank. It was believed in Westland that thought occurred in the testicles, the primary reason that the women were thought of as mere animals and property. The general would never say a word and some wondered if he could speak. One look from him was enough to assert his power and no one questioned the look. He would take out groups of men women or children at will with his heavy club of petrified wood, and he was never without it. He would point the club to give orders for all orders were simple. Kill.

The men in this culture had many wives and the higher ranking the man the more wives he would acquire. It was a militaristic society of rankings with the hierarchy beginning with slave at the bottom followed by the artisans, which consisted of the city planners, ship designers and food coordinators. The military guards were the police over the city and had all power in deciding the guilt and punishment of the lower ranks. One was always guilty and the punishment was always death. Death after torture was the harshest punishment and was reserved for the lazy and the objectors, the two worst crimes. At least half of the population of Westland was guards but they had no power over the warriors, lieutenants or the general. The only one with power over the general was the Minister of Faith, who had no name. He was a demigod and was the listener of the invisible one who made all of the laws and social ranks in Westland. It was the invisible one's greatest desire to destroy the Eastlanders or bring them under his submission as he had done long ago to the west.

General Cugat was the only general. He took his orders directly from the Minister of Faith who was directed by the invisible one. He would direct the lieutenants whose number was two thousand. There would be one or two of them to a ship and all warriors were equal. Everyone knew their job and to not fulfill it to the fullest would mean being thrown overboard for they would not eat each other out of respect.

Children as women were possessions. Children could be eaten like the women but most preferred not to eat them as to build the appetite for the children of Eastland. This was the pay for the ordinary warrior, the joys in torturing and killing the men, raping the women and young girls and eating the children without killing or cooking them first. They relished the screams of babies as they devoured their flesh. The general knew this well and he would have a cage of their own babies on each ship where one could be slain from time to time to excite the lusts of the warriors. It also was an order of the Minister of Faith and thus the commandment of the invisible one.

The ships were in the midst of The Sea and the storm was at full strength, shoving the boats as a single structure bobbing and smoking with the wail of screaming babies. The lightning would strike all around and the thunder would echo across the mountains of waves as darkness fell on the first night of blood and horror and lust. The General would take his place a third the way up the midmast, lashed to a platform on the largest of the boats, pointing his club to the east. He would be there until landfall. His thoughts were full of what he might find on a more personal level. It would be the general's right to have for him the thing that he might desire the most. He wondered if a king or a queen ruled Eastland. The last storm had destroyed a large part of the population and it was believed all of the royal family. He hoped that that wasn't true. He hoped that there was a princess or even a queen that he might defile. He hoped for the greatest prize of all for a general in a storm, a virgin queen. He daydreamed of this fetish the entire voyage and even most of his life. He would have his way with her imposing his will and brute strength. He knew how the east loved the clean and he would give her the filth. He would give her a terror and a stench of a thousand wretched beasts. He would destroy her spirit and body. He would torture her and rape her and finally he would kill her for his country and for his god, and of course, for himself.

Chapter 5

Helina

Helina was the only surviving member of the royal family of Eastland after the last storm, which was bloodier than most in recent memory. She was a fetus in her mother's womb when the west last attacked, one so horrible that seventy percent of the children were massacred along with about a third of the adult population. That storm was quick moving and caught the people by surprise. They learned much from those dark days and made better preparations over the next few decades. The primary focus would be protection of the children this time and more caves in the mountains were converted into shelters for them and an effort to hide the openings to the caves became of great importance. It was decided that for this storm the men would leave for the north to hide in the mountains after burying the children alive and sealing them into the sides of the nearby lower mountains just east of town. Rocks and boulders that would be released from above after being held in place by fallen branches and logs would close the mouths of the caves. A single cut rope would allow gravity to bring down the rubble thus burying the children deep within to where not a baby's cry could be heard. They would not be found. When the storm had passed strong men would be needed to unearth the precious cache of unharmed children. The women would use themselves as decoys and a distraction with their running and hopping to escape the marauders grasps. Many would be caught and pay the ultimate price for the warriors would be irate for the lack of babies to menace. The elders would greet the ships in costumes to confuse, misinform and buy precious time for the rest. They would be buffoon and fools and make the warriors laugh until they became bored after which they would slaughter them all.

Queen Helina would prefer to run with the women and girls but the elders talked her into hiding in the highest cave in a peak over looking the town. It was just a crevice eroded in granite with an opening just barely large enough for her to squeeze into if she exhaled. It was only large enough for one small person and she could force her body into the conch shell shaped space and no one could reach her and a torch light would not expose her. She would do, as the elders asked for she well knew that she was the last of the royal family. Her survival became a symbol for continuity for the Westlanders just as the destruction of each successive castle was a symbol for their pain, a reminder to be vigilant. It wasn't that she was more virtuous than the other women, for all of the women were virtuous and kind, as were the men. Helina had sweetness and a purity of heart that was common in her ancestors and that was a reminder to the elders of her loving father, the beloved king, whom they revered and missed so much. Nostalgia for, and a love of the dead was another of the common customs in this land where truth, grace, beauty of spirit and love abounded. Helina had the gold green eyes of her people but her hair was much darker than most. It was long and straight and shone with a reflective blue during the night and turquoise during the day. Her skin was fair and creamy, the color of the desert dunes at sunset. She was slender and athletic from running and hopping and her countenance was aglow as a result of a healthy diet and an optimistic nature. She saw only good in the world and counted each passing second of life as if it were her first and last. The childlike inquisitiveness she possessed combined with a keen wit allowed her to see each day as a new adventure that was in itself a journey to be relished and cherished. For her the cosmos stood still and observed her, as she pondered it. Certainly the men, young and old alike adored her and many would pine away at the mention of her name. Children were attracted to her as they felt that she was a kindred spirit. Old ladies hugged and kissed her and she was everyone's daughter, lover, sister, playmate, and above all, she was everyone's queen. She would do as the elders asked. She would save herself for the sake of her loving community. She would want to have children to make the royal family to continue. She saw this, as a sacrifice for nothing would be more painful then to hear the screams of the others as they would be tortured and killed. She would not be able to help them but would have to sob silently and alone in what would be her first knowledge of despair and infinite grief. She would suffer more than anyone else during the coming calamity and she would live on to feel the pain. The monster in the closet of her mind was stirring like a sleeping giant about to awaken from a dreamless slumber. She would grow in a new and undetermined direction, and her inquisitive mind found this to be very interesting indeed if not frightful. Another new feeling was also beginning to surface deep within her mind that she didn't understand at all. It was something new and she had no name for it. It was dark and cold like the mountain crevice she would soon occupy. There seemed to be a wind blowing within her body that increased steadily as the outer wind grew stronger with the approaching storm. A gale was tearing away in her mind and body that ripped apart clouds as if she were falling into an abyss. The feeling was so strong that it began to overwhelm every other thought of love and kindness. She was experiencing anger and the beginnings of hatred, a feeling never before experienced by anyone from the east. She wept at this new experience and felt dirty for the first time in her young life. She was ashamed but the intensity of the inner wind grew nonetheless. She ran to hide her face. She ran as she never ran before to the mountains, not for safety but out of shame and fear that someone would see her tears and for the first time in her life she felt ugly.

Chapter 6

Night

In the east, nighttime was quiet and mysterious. It was a time of story telling around campfires with the smells of burning driftwood. The younger people would listen to the elders pass down the tales of old about famous lovers of a thousand years ago. They new them by name as they had made a mental record of all the people of Eastland, who ever lived, even those who died at birth. This oral tradition was their history in which, every person was important. They knew the looks and mannerisms of their ancestors stretching back ten thousand years, each and every one. They knew the strengths and weaknesses of each. They knew which direction the wind blew at their births and could conjure a mental picture of the day accordingly. Even the desires and hopes of these ancient folk who lived so long ago were known. Also the patterns of the seasons and any variations in them were on record including unusual events such as when the earth shook or when the sun went dark for a few moments without a cloud in the sky. About three thousand years ago there had been the greatest shaking of the earth. It was called The Day of Chaos. That day started as any other of the days during the south wind. The water was calm and blue and the breeze was warm and the smell of salt and ice plants wafted through the town as the peaceful people laughed and kissed and went about the daily business of contemplating the wondrous world. It started with a creaking noise no one had ever heard before. It came from nowhere and everywhere. Suddenly the ground began to rumble, slowly building in vibration and noise. The water started to churn and turn a muddy brown and then the water receded completely even emptying the lagoon in a big whoosh. The land tilted towards the sea and rocks began to fall from the mountains. The ground began to sway and move in waves as large as the sea waves in a storm. Palms fell and dust flew up as everything rocked and twisted and the intensity kept growing until no one could even stand. The earth itself jumped in the air and then fell suddenly a great distance. The sea began to come back to meet the land in an enormous wave that crashed into the beach and kept coming even up to the edge of the mountains. Suddenly things fell quiet once again as the sea took its place along the beach and not a sound was heard. The water swirled slowly mixed with mud and foam and trees. When it ended there were no survivors from those who were in town and by the shore. The men and boys were on the plateau with no name and were not hurt. Some of the women were foraging in the green hills that survived as well. Many elders and women and children were lost to the sea on that terrible day so long ago. It would take only a few weeks to rebuild the homes but many generations to rebuild the population of East back to where it had been. There was a loss of innocence for a time but there was no record of those feelings or any other feelings of the survivors from that generation. It was not talked about in story time then and the tale was almost lost entirely if it were not for a few who felt it was important to pass on this story, for just as the living people loved the dead, the dead loved the not yet born.

Night was also a time for romance. Lovers would slip off into the darkness out of campfire's light. Marriage wasn't a concept but people would often mate for life and have children. It seemed to be the natural progression of things. There was no such thing as a family unit though as the children belonged to everyone. The entire town would participate in the nurturing process that would last on into adulthood and even unto death. They were all children in this respect and their innocence was obvious even in the oldest. The life span of the women was slightly more than men who often lived past a hundred years of age. Accidents were rare as they were not a reckless people and the biggest loss of life they experienced was from the attacks from the west. Every life was precious and they felt the sting of death so severely when it was violent. When someone died a natural death from aging an entire week's nights would be a time of remembering that person around the fires. The deads' presence could be felt each night and lessened until it was gone on the sixth or seventh night. It was a time of goodbyes and a time of smiles and good cheer.

Night in the west was the antithesis from the east. The fires would burn but the stories were not remembering the dead but remembering death. Tales would be told of the great campaigns against the enemy and how the invisible one had outwitted them. Night was also a time of bloodletting, torture and sacrifice to the god of the great desert. As the sun would set, the energy of the fires would inflame the lusts and passions in the folk of Westland. Women would be raped in masse by hordes of soldiers until blood flowed that would set off a frenzy of orgies of sweat and blood that would culminate in the sacrifice of anyone who might be grabbed up by the mob and beaten and burned alive. By morning the smoldering carcasses would lie about the ashes of a fire that had spread through the town and heated some of the red brick structures until they would be glowing red. There was no love making in this culture and all children were the products of rape. There was no nurturing of the children and everyone was on their own to feed themselves and to survive by the grace of the invisible one. The weak would be eaten and the cunning would become soldiers. There was much inbreeding as incestial sex was as common as any. The inbred children would be the slaves and their life span was short. A woman rarely lasted beyond childbearing years and soldiers would kill each other in angry brawls. The only reason that the culture continued was because they were so sexual. The birth rate was four times the death rate yet the population grew at a minuscule pace. Accidents were common also. The haphazard construction of their city and the disregard for the dangers of fire meant many would perish from burns or falling bricks. Rats and cockroaches were everywhere even in daylight and it was common for young children to be eaten alive by the rats as nobody cared to protect them. If they matured beyond twenty years of age they were tough indeed. Only the strong survived.

Their night was the darkest of nights and with their heathen hearts the night could not compete.

This night there were no fires except on the great ships. The desert wind blasted the sand hard through the western city and all who were in the city were holed up in their mud brick hovels. At sea the night was black as clouds obscured the starlight. The waves pushed the mass of boats, some already breaking up, towards the east. In East, preparations were under way as the wind had already blown away most of the houses of palm and driftwood. The children were being secured in the caves and the elders were rehearsing. Gathering up their costumes, the women were drinking a sugary drink made from nuts that would give them energy for the chase. Queen Helina oversaw the operations from her mountain peak as the hatred was growing within her. Her heart knew anger and violence. She contemplated murder as she bit down on her teeth and strained as though she lifted a heavy weight. It was the darkest night that anyone could remember and for Helina it was so dark that the world disappeared from her vision, as she turned inward to the darkness in her mind. Her inner light had become so dim that it was as a star so far away and faint that its light could not reach the earth on the clearest of nights. She crawled into the tiny cave to escape the increasing wind but it whistled at the opening and it sounded like a dying woman. She did not hear it for deep within her mind and heart there was only silence and darkness.

Chapter 7

The Elders

During the long dark night the people of Eastland were preparing for the test of their lives. It would be a time unlike any that they had known, with the rushing about in preparation for what was to come and the logistics were overwhelming. They knew not when the boats would arrive but the best guess of the eldest of the elders, Jaaken, was another full day with landfall perhaps at dawn. His calculations of the wind and how quickly it intensified would bring the boats at a much more rapid pace than the last storm. Jaaken was one hundred and fifteen years old and he had lived through three previous attacks. This was to be his forth and there was not another in the stories of old who had survived four. He knew this well as he was the master storyteller and had a keen mind still at his advanced age. He would forget unimportant things like eating or sleeping but he never forgot a name and had committed to memory the names of all who had ever lived since storytelling began. He was the archive of the community and everyone would come to him when there were questions about lineage or even what the weather was like when a person was born. He was the leader of the elders by default because of his age but he was also the source of facts when there was confusion or debate about the history of East.

Jaaken knew that this storm would be a particularly bad one and the way the weather was behaving, perhaps the worst in history. That was troublesome for him and the urgency in his directions to the others made even him a bit nervous, but there was something else that made him apprehensive. He was concerned about Helina, for he knew more about the last storm than he'd told. He held a secret in his heart for twenty years from that terrible time. It was locked away inside his mind of facts that he dared not share at the story telling. His thoughts were on the royal family and how they had been destroyed. The beloved King Jasper was burned alive in front of the castle while his queen looked on. All of the children of the king were eaten alive and his wife, Queen Reena was raped by the general in front of his eyes as he burned. His last word was commanding her to "Run", as he perished. Jaaken saw all of this from a hole in the sand he had dug for himself as to witness the events. That was his purpose. He had seen the queen break free and run for her life to the plateau with no name with the general in pursuit. He never caught her but he'd had the pleasure of raping her anyway and in front of the burning king. Queen Reena survived and became pregnant. She would have the daughter she would name Helina, which has a dual meaning, "Light", and "Fire". It was assumed by all that she was the daughter of the King's, and Jaaken would pass along the story to all that this was so, especially to Helina. Queen Reena died a few months after the birth of her daughter in a rare and tragic accident by falling from a cliff on the highest peak of the nearby mountains. The same peak where Queen Helina was now hiding in the conch shaped tiny cave. She did not know that this was the very place of her mother's death.

The elders were preparing for the attack as if for a performance. They had taken refuge from the wind in the castle and were arranging their costumes and practicing lines. The only art form that existed in the east was storytelling. The logical next step was theater, and the elders were developing it during story time by the fire as a diversion and a game of learning. They would make up outrageous stories of the dead that couldn't possibly be true to entertain the folks and to make them laugh. The Eastlanders loved to laugh. They laughed at the absurdity of stories of ancestors with feathered wings who could fly or others who lived beneath the sea and could breathe water. There were even stories of invisible people who would play all manner of trickery on the visible ones. It would help the younger to remember the true stories by contrasting fantasy and all had a fine time in the process. The elders would now use their new theater to slow down the monsters with laughter it was hoped. It was thought that the west had no laughter and if they didn't, it did not matter for their pace would be hindered by the mere presence of the actors and they would most likely die a swift death. For this reason a number of the elders would be hiding under rocks or in high grass to be witnesses to all that would happen during the storm as well as to survive to pass on the knowledge of the past.

There was electricity in the air both from lightning and from the excitement of opening night for the troupe. For the first time they were taking their show on the road and it would be a tough crowd.

There were a variety of costumes in the group that were characters from the fantasy tales that were told. One dressed as a feathered creature using grass and palms to make the wings. Short grass clippings were all over his body attached with mud. Another had painted his body like fish scales using pigment from the ashes of a fire and dandelions flowers. This was the first example of body decoration among the peoples of either culture and was the beginning of painting. Many had carved masks from tree bark with large smiling faces and eyes made from seashells. This was the first sculpture that anyone could remember. Another of the elders had decided to climb a tall palm tree just as the big ships arrived. He would tie dead fronds around himself as camouflage and lash his body to near the top so the wind would not blow him down. He created a cone from a conch so his voice could be heard over the cacophony. He would represent an invisible one from the entertaining stories. The elders were taking great pleasure in the idea of a farce as there whole beings evolved around truths. This was not a farce of lies but rather one of survival. It would obey the two social rules of the culture, to hurt no one, and to survive. Art had crept into this culture out of necessity. Its beginnings were games and it had, in a very short time, evolved into a weapon.

It was a time of upheaval for Eastland but the only one aware of this was Jaaken. He knew of the queen's origin and he initiated the changes in how story telling was done. He saw how she was changing during this crises and he saw how the fantasies were being used for a purpose other than informing. He knew that the entire earth was about to be altered forever but he couldn't predict just how extensive the difference would be or what lie in the future. He was wise and insightful and perceived the transformation of the world through the winds of change that was upon them. He was excited and remorseful as he felt fear himself for the first time. It was also a fear of the unknown. He was reserved and cheerful among his comrades and they would never know his feelings as the troupe readied the farce.

Chapter 8

The Children

    The loving and gentle children were being brought to the caves by the women as the men were checking the ropes and log that held up the small avalanches, which would seal them within. The women laughed and joked as the children giggled with glee at the adventure. They knew that they would be entombed and they knew that they would be separated from the rest of the people and they also knew not for how long. The children of East were trusting for they understood the depth of the love that the people felt for them. They were the light of the day and the whisper of night. The sounds of their voices were the only music in the world. The hopes of their lives were the reason for breathing and the sweetness of their spirits always inspired the old. All the towns' efforts were for them, for they were the continuation of all things. They were the stories and they would carry on the ideologies of existing in the world to enjoy sunsets and to kiss one another after sneaking away from the fires. Without them the people would die and the culture of love, hope and sweetness would pass away forever. Even the howling wind and thunderous clouds could not dampen the moment of sweetness of separation. The Eastlanders would cry for joy when parting ways and would cry again when reunited. The deep connectedness they felt for each other was not diminished by time, just as the girls were taught that wanting is sometimes better than having. They all knew that the children would be safe and the children understood the patience of waiting for reunification. In the meantime they would have each other.

The children of West were miniatures of the adults. They were born with a full set of sharp teeth and would crave raw flesh within a week of life. It was not uncommon for babies to eat their mother's nipples and it was not unheard of for a woman to die from a fetus eating her while still in the womb. They were born into a cruel and filthy world of suffering and torment. They were lusty cannibals and many would die from neglect, abuse or ending up as food for adults. There was no teaching. All in the western culture was base instinct and responding to the environment, which was most despicable. Most were the product of rape or incest and none had a family structure with siblings unless it was a coincidence. Each child was expendable and they loathed each other, as jealousy was the first emotion to surface. If one were too deformed from inbreeding they would be fuel for fire or simply left to the rats, as they were not worthy for food. When they were in adolescence they would run in packs like wild hyenas, preying on the old and sick. They roamed the back alleys and fought amongst themselves when no one else was around. They drank fermented blood and raped passers by, male or female. The girls were indistinguishable from the boys in their ruthlessness and savage appetites. They could fight with the boys and some gangs had a female leader because she was the meanest one. The city was divided into territories where the all night wars would rage on the fringes of the adult orgies. Sometimes the gangs would be swept up into the fornication and murder of the adult frenzies and the result would be burnt or pregnant children. Many girls would die as a result of being physically unfit to handle the bearing of a baby that could reach half her weight before delivery and the fetus generally would eat them from the inside out. The children would sleep down by the red clay beaches where corpses and refuse washed ashore. Their hair was never cut and always filled with blood from lying under the docks of the shipbuilding lagoon. When the survivors matured physically they would take their places in society as slaves or soldiers. The desirable females would become property and the rest would become the food for dogs. It was a miserable and wretched life from the womb until death, but it was all that the peoples of West had ever known. It was the will of the invisible one for he created all things, and all things were as they should be.

The children of the east were as innocent as trees bending in the wind. In the same respect so were the children of the west. Is a tiger to blame for killing a doe or a flounder the perch? These children were the same as any other child in nature. They were born to have certain characteristics as is the tiger and the flounder. The difference is cultural to some degree. Certainly the Eastland child, who grows up with love and in an environment where all life is sacred, will become lovers and soft walkers on the earth. Pity the child from Westland. This is a beast of the wild that grows in an unforgiving desert so empty that the thought of nourishment never surfaces. It lives in a land, which is as black and empty as the vacuum of space without stars. The word hope has no meaning and the word joy means savage lust. The idea of the invisible one has caused the dark side of life to completely overshadow its counterpart, light. A nature out of balance created by the intellect of nature itself. Eastland children not having the invisible one are blind to the darkness and see only the light. They also are a nature out of balance by the virtue of ignorance. They do not hate the darkness for they have never experienced it and know not what to hate. They only understand love and even love for those who dwell in darkness and have only hate in their hearts. The East was a universe apart from the west, polarized by their different natures. They each understand only one thing and that is what makes them the same. They are the flip side of the coin from each other, one always facing away from the other, always looking inward and never seeing the other and never to understand the other. One is love and the other is hate.

They had the children placed deep within the caves and the men pulled the ropes simultaneously and the rocks and boulders tumbled down to seal the entrances. The last thing they heard was their laughter, then silence and the sound of the wind.

Chapter 9

The Morning

The men made there way in darkness and wind to the northern mountains to wait out the event. It was difficult for them to leave but they knew that there was no other way. Their thoughts were of survival now and for one reason alone. The children would need to be excavated as soon as possible when the enemy would finally leave. They would not be pursued, as the soldiers would exhaust their energies chasing the females. Then the wind would begin to shift direction and they would be forced to leave. There was no record of the Westlanders remaining even by accident, as they would take their chances making their way back across the sea even if it would mean being stranded and blown off course. They hated the eastern shores with its pristine beaches and lovely landscape. They hated the clean of it all and they especially hated it in the day when it would sparkle like dappled sunlight on a rippled pond. The morning was the worst time for them as it was a time for sleeping off the black night of violence and lust. The men of East adored the morning with nature's intense colors at sunrise and the dew on the blue grass steaming up to meet the sun's rays which shone like spotlights through low slung morning clouds that were making their way down to the water's edge. For them it was a time of shining. Everyone in East liked to shine from time to time. They would clean themselves in the spring or waterfall that made it's way down from the snow-capped mountains to the east. They would smile and beam the joy of love and tenderness on all the happy people like a cluster of morning stars. It was how they started each day followed by many group hugs and kisses even before breakfast. The western heathens hid their bloody and bruised faces at first light. Not from shame for they knew not the meaning, but to escape from light of day and thus ruin the darkness that was within them. They would cling to blackness so dark and foul and in their minds, was not a spark of awareness or emotion beyond hate, lust, or wanting, which crowded out all things lovely. They were the walking and breathing dead and they abhorred life. They were completely miserable but knew nothing else, they were satisfied in their own blackness. The morning was a time of sleep. Sleep at sea was impossible. The log ships rocked and rolled on the wind blasted waves at sunrise. There was barely a difference from night to day for the boiling clouds blotted out the sun. The on board fires were extinguished by water crashing onto the decks and most of the barrels of blood were gone. Many of the soldiers had been lost during the night but no one seemed to notice. There was no conversation and the general was still lashed to his post pointing his petrified club to the east. He realized their speed of travel and determined that they would make landfall by the following dawn. The storm was severe and he'd hoped that there would be enough of the boats and men left to carry on their determined destruction and violence. The day would intensify the storm but they were on the leading edge of it riding the mountainous waves. The breath of God would guide them to their destiny and to glory.

When the men were coming into the foothills of the northern mountains the sun's first rays shone gloriously up over the high ridge to their east. It was clear to the east but when they made their way up beyond the tree line and looked to the west they saw a boiling gray sea. The edge of the storm was below them as they could see a great distance and beyond that the sky and water merged into blackness. As the sun finally peeked over the peak, a fantastic sight they beheld. The light lit up the high white tops of the storm clouds with colors of green and gold. Above them the pale blue sky was empty and silent, peaceful. The winds were gusting fiercely at this high altitude and they were bitter cold and went on to seek shelter to wait for the storm to pass. They would not speak nor even look at each other for there was nothing to say, nothing to do but wait.

The children were alone in the damp caves and the darkness was absolute. They could not have fires for warmth or light for even if there were chimneys the smoke or a crying baby would give them away. They had each other and this was essential for their survival, both emotionally and physically. The entrances were sufficiently covered to where a sound could not be heard from the outside world, especially in the wind. They would sit close and when one became chilled the others would place the cold child at the center of the group. The community was a collective and now that the children were separated they became a collective unto themselves. The older ones would comfort the others with stories that they had remembered from the fires, dwelling on the tales that were funny or lovely. They imagined the dawn outside as the eldest child whose name was Mik, described in vivid detail his favorite sunrise. It was an unforgettable event when everything in the universe was in tune. Standing on the blue hills he remembered looking out to sea as the suns light came from behind him and the mountains. It was during the south wind when the water was aquamarine blue and clear. The rays of light were reflected off the sky and on to the sea. The sea would then reflect the light to the shore and back up to the sky. The result was an unbelievably dazzling display of a multitude of shimmering colors that changed with each passing second. The water was calm and the south wind was softly blowing warm wind through his hair. The experience left him breathless and almost giddy for the whole of the day. It was etched in his mind's eye and he had longed to express his feelings about it but never found the right time to tell it until now. He had a captive as well as a captivated audience. The children had been up the whole night and this story lulled them gently to sleep where they all dreamed the same dream of coming out of the cave into that very sunrise. They dreamed that they were all flying together as a flock of seagulls over the beaches and waves. They dreamed of being reborn into a new life of light and love, and when they awoke within the cave later that day they would all be comforted.

The anxiety among the women and girls was almost unbearable. In their preparations for this time they were preoccupied with helping to secure the children and saying their goodbyes to the men. They had made their way onto the plateau with no name and by the edge of the black forest. They had a small fire going beside a low ridge and sat silently contemplating the events to come. In their minds was the intense concentration of athletes before the competition, going over the chase again and again. They knew that many of them would die as they rested leaning one upon the other. They cried silently as the early morning sun's rays penetrated the trees and cast dimly upon their hair and shoulders.

In her little cave Helina was drawn out the dark recesses of her mind by the light reflecting around the curve of the conch shaped wall that slowly illuminated the smooth stone to match the color of her sand colored skin. The brighter it got the more her thoughts became focused on the present and she heard the whistling wind. She walked to the entrance and held her hands up in defiance, as if she were pushing the wind like a great weight. Anger blazed up in her like an inferno and she knew that she would fight. She would fight the mighty storm that was coming and she knew that she would fight to the death. She had never felt this before nor had anyone in East. Her eyes were glazed over and dilated until they became as black as her hair. She began to breath heavy as the rage grew to the point where she screamed a yell loud and long and the elders heard it as it echo from the mountains to the sea. Jaakens' hair stood on end and he knew immediately the meaning in her voice and he was afraid. The sun's heat brought with it the first of the rains, and the wind grew steadily.

Chapter 10

The Rain

    The morning sun was climbing as the first clouds arrived on shore. A fine salt spray glistened and swirled in the wind while the day was still bright with diffused light. Each moment the mist grew thicker and the day grew darker as the wind intensified. Large droplets of rain spattered on the beach and the pattern that they created in the sand slowly disappeared as the water ran down to the sea. The sky darkened to a deep gray as the storm's leading edge made its way inland. At sea the great ships were approaching but still a good half-day away. The fleet had been decimated by a night of crashing waves. All of the smaller boats had vanished while just half of the largest remained, many of them broken and smashed. The storm had been merciless and the waves were so violent that logs shot straight up in the air completely clearing the towering waves, and then crashing down on the vessels again and again causing damage all the while. The rains became blinding solid sheets of water a foot thick that was blown at tremendous speed. Not a soul was on the decks except the general whose perch was high enough to miss the waves washing over the tops of the ships. He was soaked and slapped by the driving vertical waves of rain but it seemed not to affect him. He was bleeding from the lashes that kept him tied to the main mast and the deer's head on his boulders thrashed about. He looked like a two-headed beast tied to a stake struggling to escape the slaughter. He pointed his club to the east from time to time as to remind himself of his purpose.

The elders sought refuge in the castle as the heavy rains began to pour in through the roof made of tar covered ancient timbers. They were resting and some were even snoring. Suddenly a crack of lightning followed by thunder booming through the hills startled them awake. They climbed up on stone ledges along the inner wall of the castle that served as a high walk above the mud floor. A few timbers from the roof were blown off by a gust of wind and rain and the water cascaded in. They managed to keep dry as rivers fell from the ceiling and it seemed as though they were in the backside of a small waterfall. They took great pains to keep their costumes as dry as possible for fear that they would disintegrate. All that they could do is wait and took turns climbing to the top window to look out to sea for the first sign of the ships. The castle was not a fortress but it could withstand a fair amount of what the sky and sea could give. They would be safe from the lightning that flashed and crashed all around them until the landing of the Westlanders and then they would be ready.

The rain came down in torrents so strong that the palms were soon stripped bare. The waves came crashing higher and met the streams flowing down to meet them in whirling pools as the beach disappeared. The only cemetery in East was on the plateau. It looked like a lake with tiny pyramid shaped islands of piled stone equally spaced and pointing to the sky. The Eastlanders revered the dead and respected their remains and unlike the west where corpses were eaten and the bones discarded, they buried them in deep graves after carefully wrapping them in banana leaves. They would include an object most cherished by the deceased such as a string of shells or some of their favorite flowers. They did not ponder an afterlife and thought only of them as living in stories. The words in this culture were the continuance of everything that they were, including individuals. As long as they lived on in stories, they lived. Helina peeked out from her cave and saw the lake of pyramids below. Her hair quickly became soaked as she watched the little waves wash against the tiny islands and thought about the dead. She thought about the future and was determined that the stories of her culture would live on. She knew in her heart that somehow, some way her people would survive this encroaching catastrophe. She made up her mind then and there to live so that the dead might live. She knew that she alone would protect her people and their history and for the first time she considered the after life. She thought of the dead as still living, not just in words but also in reality. They were counting on her to protect them for as long as there was someone living in her world, they could live forever. Eternity.

Chapter 11

The Landing

   The general saw a break in the clouds before him and
caught a glimpse of the mountains of East. He screamed with
delight but no one could hear him over the sound of the
deafening wind and waves. He cut his bonds and scurried
down from the mast to gather his troops to ready the ships
for grounding. Only the largest of the log boats had survived
the perilous crossing and more than half of the men were
lost. They would have plenty of soldiers to do the job and
several were below decks preparing for the attack. The
largest ship had a long room that was being used for target
practice with a new weapon that was developed recently by
the Minister of Faith. A crude bow and arrow would give the
soldiers the edge that they needed in chasing the young
women of East. They knew that the girls were fast and
furious runners with uncanny jumping abilities and in recent
months a special force of archers had been training on deer.
The weapon was a secret known only to the general and a
few lieutenants but was now being shown for the first time to
the soldiers. They were afraid at the speed of the shaft of
wood and saw it as being a gift of the invisible one. The
archers were training themselves to aim for the runners' legs,
to cripple them and to make them easy prey for the raping.
The soldiers would still use traditional clubs to murder the
elders and any men that they would encounter. It was difficult
to shoot the arrows on the rocking ship and most missed the
mark and at times a bystander would take a shaft of wood

through the head, which brought great delight to all. They were drinking fermented blood and a killing frenzy began on board before the landing that culminated with a slaughter of the remaining caged babies of their own until none were alive. The soldiers were ankle deep in fresh blood that sloshed about until all were covered head to toe. The animal skins they wore turned crimson and blood dripped from their long hair and teeth. The biggest ship suddenly bumped the sea bottom and lurched forward a few times until it came to a halt rocking with the pounding waves. The other boats followed in succession from the larger to the smaller and progressively rested nearer to shore. Ropes fell from the sides and the men made their way en masse to the beaches of Eastland. Loose logs were falling into the water from the boats and many soldiers held on for a ride in on the waves. They were not good swimmers but the water was only knee deep in the valley of the waves but was twenty or so feet when the crests broke by them. Most would be ashore in short order for they relied on their brute strength to fight their way to the land.

The elders had not seen the ships masts approaching for the rain made them invisible, and before they knew it they heard the crashing and creaking of the lumbering behemoths as they beached. The first thing they saw was a horde of half animal looking giants coming headlong through the waves on foot and surfing the logs towards them. They were frightened and wanted to run but they gathered their wits and rushed out to greet the barbarians dressed in costumes and acting as buffoons. The warriors saw them and were bewildered at first but the pre attack frenzy had them so worked up to kill what ever moved and the elders were crushed by an onslaught of swinging clubs in a matter of seconds. The elders died in this their first performance of the stage. No one would appreciate the costumes or wonder at the dialog. There would be no encore and for that matter there would be no applause. It would have been a bloody affair but the driving rain diluted all traces of red as the elders lay mutilated in the mud. The general took a quick glance around and then pointed his club to the blue grass hills. The army followed him in a disorderly gang of collective animal spirits as they marched steadily towards the next victims. At that moment an unprecedented thing happened. The wind began to die at a fast rate until there was none at all. The rain continued in a torrential downpour straight to the ground. This confounded the general for he understood what should be happening but it was not. The storm should have intensified behind him until the wind direction shifted back to the west. The waves began to subside until only the momentum of the rocking sea kept the surf rolling in. The storm was dying. His thoughts turned to the return home and how they would be stranded in East if the back pressure from the storm didn't happen, to blow his ships back to sea. It only stopped the men for a moment as he commenced his charge inland, up the slippery slopes towards the hills and the plateau. He knew that the rest of the Eastlanders would be there and his thoughts of murder and rape over powered all other thoughts. He would confront the weather problem later but for now the joy of the chase was first and foremost in his mind.

Helina looked out from her cave and marveled at the subsidence of the wind. She went out to let the fresh rain water pour over her body. She could barely make out the tiny figures working their way uphill from the beach like tiny ants clamoring over a dead corpse. She noticed that there was not as many ships as she'd expected, perhaps a hundred. She guessed that there was as many as twenty thousand soldiers. For the first time since the storm began she began to feel hope. They were not out numbered but they were certainly out matched. She knew that she could not count on the men of her culture for help in trying to defeat this monstrous plague for they were not killers. It would be in violation of their time honored code, even if it meant the death of all of the children. She was sure that the children would be safe, but she worried about the men and women. The girls and women had a chance of survival in the running, but she feared for the men, as they would now probably make their way back from the North Mountains thinking that the storm had died before the landing. She thought that they would all be killed as she slipped back into her cave to plan on what to do next. The rain began to slow to a steady drizzle and she could barely hear the soldiers' shouts that were struggling up through the mud to the blue hills. Suddenly her dark cave became amber yellow as a single shaft of sunlight beamed through the clouds and struck the cave's entrance. It startled her so that she ran out to greet it with open arms, and the heat from the ray bathed her face. She stood on this high peak, lit up like a vision in the midst of darkness and the soldiers took no notice for they were busy negotiating the slopes. The rain turned to a fine mist and her thoughts became clear. Her spirit soared with an awakening unlike anything she had ever experienced. She thought that there must be an underlying force at work that she could not explain. She was exalted and felt weightless in the midst of the tragedy of her life. She stared at the sun through this tiny opening in the clouds and spoke to it as if it were her father. "Sun", she uttered, "You are my father!" She knew in her heart that this sun, this orb in the sky that had always come to warm her day, that would disappear in the evening and would always return. This, the thing that she took for granted was not a thing but a being who cared for her. This being who had watched her all of her life was now her savior. This light in the sky had become the light in her heart, and her insides became an inferno of hope and bravery. He had always been there and now he would show her the way and protect her. The beam of light stayed on her for the longest time even as the clouds moved the light remained. Jaaken saw this incredible vision from afar, perched in his palm tree on the beach where he had lashed himself, hidden from the view of the soldiers as they landed. He was the sole survivor of the elders and he had witnessed the monsters bloody rampage that took his friends' lives. He was now a witness to this transfiguration of the queen. It was a religious experience for her and the phenomenon he observed touched him someplace new, even with his decades of wisdom. He had witnessed three storms before this one and never had the wind and rain stopped so soon. He had seen much carnage and had recorded the atrocities that the west had inflicted, and it wasn't uncommon for members of the royal family to stand before the soldiers and die without fear. Queen Helina was different. He knew who her father was and he saw him close on this day once more. It was the general who looked older and meaner but he knew him by his posturing in the blinding rain and wind as he landed. He looked him in the face unseen from above but the barbarian looked right through him without noticing him. Jaaken Was astonished at these turns of events as the history of his people was playing out before his eyes, and he knew that this would be a unique and profound day, but still he could not predict what might happen. How would this newfound strength of the queen's come to fruition and how would this occupation end, but most of all what would become of Eastland?

The mass of soldiers reached the hills and raced for the plateau with no name. The girls panicked and scattered in all directions, jumping and sliding in the mud. Twenty thousand beasts with long hair flying and clubs and genitalia swinging chased the females without much success. Suddenly the groups of archers appeared from behind a ridge to the south and let loose with several volleys of arrows hitting many bare legs and ankles. The girls fell by the dozens and were caught up by the mob that made quick work of their duties. The new weapons set off a stampede of women and girls into the dark forest where soldiers continued the chase until the woods became so thick that there was no escape for them. They could not run and jump in the thicket and the archers pulled up from the rear to wound every leg. This would be the end of the women of Eastland accept for the queen and the female children. Many mothers and virgins died in a matter of moments after being raped repeatedly.

Helina saw all of this from her lookout. The inferno in her grew into a thousand suns. The energy of the sun himself was within her body and he was angered by the crimes committed against his children.

The men of East had been traveling happily down from the north when they came upon this bloody spectacle. They were all killed at once in a massacre that left them torn to pieces. Helina watched as thousands of her men and boys were slaughtered on the top of one of the blue hills. Rivers of red ran down the blue grass until the hill turned purple. She would never forget this color she thought as she fainted from grief and fell back into her cave were she would remain unconscious for the rest of the day.

Jaaken slid down from the palm where he was perched and made his way undetected north up the beach to where he could follow the lagoon to the waterfall and climb up the mountain peak to meet up with Helina. He was an old man with aching joints but he was still able to run and climb at a slower pace than when he was young, but he would reach her in due time. All that he could think of was the vision he had witnessed and what it all could mean. Being the most knowledgeable of his people he went over in his mind all the stories from the history of special events but he could not remember anything quite like what had just happened with Helina. He thought about the bravery of King Jasper as he burned and he thought about Helina's mother, as he knew that her death was a suicide. None knew beside him, not even Helina. He could not be positive that it wasn't an accident but all of the evidence pointed to the former, as she was distraught since her rape by the general from West. She had never confided in him or anyone else about it but she was never the same. Jaaken was convinced that Queen Reena was killed by the general as sure as he was that Helina was the general's child. He would do his best to make sure that Helina never found out the ugly truth of her conception as he feared that she would suffer the same fate as her mother and become yet another victim of this horrible monster. He knew that she was a blend of the east and the west but he had no idea just what it would mean for Helina and her people. He only knew that he would help her in whatever way possible and he knew that he would be silent concerning her true father and she would never know this truth.

After the soldiers finished smashing the bodies of the men into pieces with their clubs, they started looking around for where the children might be hidden. The general realized that the caves would be the obvious hiding places and commanded his men to search them all until they were discovered. The clouds had begun to roll away to the north and the general knew that they were stranded. Most of the soldiers were unaware of this situation as they were focused on their lusts and hatred so that they seemed to not even notice that the storm had subsided. It was the first campaign for all but the general, some lieutenants and a handful of soldiers. The great army was young and full of animal spirit with a thirst for blood that would not be easily quenched. They became so wild that the general didn't try to control them but rather just laughed for the first time in his life. His thoughts were on the royal family and the possibility of finding the queen. He did not know Reena by name but remembered the great pleasure that he took with her as her husband watched and burned. That was his fondest memory in life and if he could repeat such a scenario on this invasion, he would be satisfied. He knew that Queen Reena would be twenty years older but perhaps she had a young daughter or two that he could destroy. Even if she were childless he would be happy to repeat his duties with her once again, perhaps with a new king to burn. He looked about in all directions contemplating where Reena might have hidden herself. He felt certain that she was near for she would want to observe the unfolding events. She would not flee to the mountains to the north or down the beach to the south. She would have been spotted with the girls in the woods and she would most certainly separate herself from the children just to protect them. The general wasn't just speculating but something else told him that she was near and watching him. As he panned the landscape with his keen eyes he spotted Jaaken climbing up the highest peak to the east. Had he not been intently looking he would have missed him all together. He left his troops to scour the open caves as he quietly slipped away down a hill to find the base of the mountain where the elder was climbing. He did not run but went at a casual pace for there was no hurry. The east wind would not come to carry him home and the old man climbing the peak would be there when he arrived.

The soldiers had made quick searches of the open caves to find no one hiding. The men became quarrelsome and begun to fight each other when one of the lieutenants noticed some recent landslides where piles of ruble had collected half way up one of the small mountains. He ordered the troops to move some stones aside to see if the rocks concealed a cave opening. A few of the men began to complain about the menial labor when suddenly the rest of the soldiers attacked and killed them in an instant. For to show contempt to orders was an automatic death sentence and is carried out without debate by the rest of the collective. Their blood lust was the driving force behind the murders, not for the blood of the killed but for the children's. They were just in the way and the sooner the problem was disposed of the sooner they would attain their goal. They all worked feverishly heaving stones large and small down the mountainside until a slow avalanche was created as the pile became smaller. There was blood everywhere from their knuckles thrashing and grappling the rocks, some of which took three or four strong men to lift. All of the thousands of soldiers were gathered on that precarious slope working as one in such haste that they paid no attention to the mountain beginning to give way beneath them. Helina looked on at the spectacle and shouted at them but their grunts and cheering drowned out her voice. She knew that this was one of the main caves where many hundreds of children would soon be unearthed. They were in grave danger and she cried out to the sun for help in this, the darkest hour. Jaaken arrived at her side at that moment after his long climb and he joined her in beseeching the sun for help out of sheer desperation if not out of faith. The general quickened his pace up the mountain to get to who he thought was Queen Reena. He heard a low rumbling noise echoing through the peaks, which became progressively louder. At that moment the sun started getting dark when there were no clouds to obscure it. All eyes turned to face it and saw that it was dissolving away from left to right until it was gone and a black hole was left in its place. Despair flooded into Helina's body like water in an empty vessel at this sight for she believed that her father, the sun had forsaken her in her hour of need. All of the soldiers had stopped and were staring at the gaping black hole in the sky but were not fearful. It meant nothing to them. The rumbling mountain began to give way under their feet, slowly at first, then suddenly the entire area on which they stood fell in an instant and twenty thousand men rolled down the mountain churning in a whirl of boulders and stones accompanied by a mighty wind all the way to the bottom. There rested a bloody heap of flesh and rock with no survivors. Helina was in shock, Jaaken began to sob and the general screamed in the silence of the aftermath that echoed for what seemed like an eternity. The sun's light began to return and illuminated the catastrophe in its full glory. The entire face of the mountain was gone and a cliff remained where the men had been working to remove the ruble from the cave entrance. A baby's cry filled the air followed by the sound of hysterical children. The cave was open and the boys and the girls were walking out of the darkness and into the light of the overhanging cliff. The children were saved and the monsters of evil were gone. Helina and Jaaken fell to their knees and worshipped the sun, their father and savior of the children. He had delivered them from evil in their moment of doubt and despair. Helina knew that god existed and he was benevolent and loving of her people. Her culture for so long had no god, no savior, and no loving entity in the sky that cared for them. She knew that he had always been there, to warm their bodies and light the darkness. She would never doubt him again for he was all knowing and all caring.

The general reached the peak where Helina and Jaaken stood. His only thoughts were murder. The rape of a queen was far from his mind after witnessing the destruction of his army. Helina pulled at Jaaken's arm to get him into her little conch shaped cave to escape the bloody monster that lurched for them but Jaaken pushed her into the cave and positioned himself on the edge of the cliff. The general passed him by and tried to squeeze himself into the small opening to get to the queen to kill her. He thought it was Reena and his goal was to finish her off before killing the elder. He reached in with his long arm and tore at her clothes and hair. She pressed herself tight against the back of the cave and when she inhaled he could touch her breasts with his fingertips. He tore out a tuft of her hair and lunged in once more to get a grip on her flesh to extricate her from her shell. Jaaken was yelling and crying behind the general and begged him to kill him instead. The general became annoyed with this and turned to push him off of the high precipice to be rid of him. The old man was not weak and grabbed on to the general with all of his might. At that moment Helina's rage overtook her and she launched out of the cave, pushing her strong legs against the back wall and propelled herself into the general and Jaaken with the force of an attacking tiger. The men in their tight embrace were knocked off balance and fell a thousand feet to their deaths while the general bit Jaaken and pulled out his arms and hair. They fell a great distance until they crashed against the rocky wall again and again until their bodies exploded on a large boulder at the base of the mountain. She cried softly for Jaaken while remembering all that he'd taught her since she was a baby. He was her favorite elder with his kind eyes and soft voice. She knew that he cared for her in the way a father would. He had now given his life for her and she would always remember him sitting around the fires on cool evenings, telling the tales of old while she laid on her back and watched the stars. Now he was gone forever from this world but she would continue to feel his spirit with her for the rest of her life. She thought of these things and pushed out of her mind the fact that she had just killed. She was the first Eastlander to take a life even out of self-defense. Her mind blocked this and she would now tend to the children for they were all that was left of her people. The elders, the women and the men all were gone. The sun had defeated the enemy and all that she could think of to do was to gather the children and leave this country. Leave their home that was everything to her culture. Leave their history and loved ones behind forever. Never again will they face the awful demons from the west. They would travel far away to where they would not be found and start their world, her world a new.

Chapter 12

The Leaving

Queen Helina descended the mountain slowly to gather her thoughts. She heard the children crying out to her but she didn't look in their direction, not because she was unaware of their plight but because she was engrossed in her thoughts about the future. She knew that she would bring the children down from their cliff and gather them together to make plans to dig out the remaining two caves where the remaining citizens of West were entombed. It would be a difficult task but her determination and compassion would drive her on. She stopped for a moment and looked up to the sun. She had no doubts about the future then for her great father in the sky was her protector and guide. Things would work themselves out and she would know where to take the children when it was time to leave. The sun was speaking to her like a voice coming from within her and his warmth comforted her.

She reached the bottom of her mountain and went straight away climbing up to the cliff where the massive landslide had happened. The rubble provided her with a stairway up the side to nearly where the children where gathered. She could see the sun over the peak while climbing as its rays seemed to light a pathway up the slope to greet it. She stopped once again to view the flooded cemetery with its pointed islands of stone placed equidistant apart and saw the suns reflection in the still waters. Each lIttle pyramid of stone lit up in a golden hue from reflecting the light off of the water. Here lie the dead whom she loved and remembered. She thought about the recently killed members of her culture and decided that each and every one must have the pyramid of stones placed on their bodies to honor their lives and as a symbol to represent her ascent up this mountain to the children and the living. She was climbing so that her people could live on forever and the sun was pulling her and pushing her at the same time, up this stairway to eternity and to him. Her experience was profound and her ideas were absurd but the moment was real and not some dream or story. She knew that she was living a very important moment and her consciousness was elevated more the higher she climbed. When she reached the happy children they drowned her with hugs and kisses as they all embraced and bathed in the warmth of the glow of the sun. They cried and laughed as one spirit in a frozen moment of ecstasy and sorrow. She grabbed up the smallest baby in her hands and pushed it to the sun and exclaimed, "Father, these are your children whom you have saved. They shall follow you for eternity for you are eternal. We will dedicate our lives to you for we are weak little children and you are the all knowing and all loving father we never knew. We know you now!"

During this moment of enlightenment she glanced down to the sea. There were the masses of lumber boats rocking gently in the surf, stuck with their bottoms in the sand. She became overwhelmed with the sense of urgency at this sight as the fear of the monsters of west rose up to her throat and almost chocked her. How could she be sure that there were not other ships anchored far off shore and many soldiers were making their way paddling in smaller log boats? The immediacy of this possibility made her urge the children down from the cliff and they proceeded to unearth other survivors from the caves. They struggled for hours, lifting stones and digging with their hands until they were bloodied. She realized that without the men it was an impossible task but all the men had perished.

They all gathered at the lagoon to clean themselves at sunset while they wept. She had thought long about which direction to leave their country behind. She knew that the cool air came from the north and to the east was the impenetrable forest. She would take the children south along the beach. People had traveled in that direction before and it was known that in a week's walk there was a rocky outcrop that jutted out into the sea. That was as far as anyone ever went before, as it was a virtual wall, higher than the tallest palm. She was listening to her inner voice of the sun and this was the direction that he chose. They left behind the buried children and the unburied corpses in their haste, and this would haunt her dreams for many nights to come. There was nothing to gather in the way of food and clothing for the storm had destroyed everything. They started the journey at a trot down the beach, led by Queen Helina followed by the youngest girls. Next were the older girls who carried the babies in their arms. The youngest boys followed and in the end of the caravan were the eldest boys to pick up the stragglers and to watch the rear. Helina held the smallest baby tight to her bosom as she picked up the pace. The fright within her made her feet move faster and she ran at a full sprint for a time like she was on fire. The children screamed for her to wait and she fell to her knees on the moonlit sand and broke down into the deep sobbing and moaning of a grieving mother. The children all comforted her in her despair until she was able to stand and start a steady pace, walking to the south as she would for the next many months, walking with no destiny in mind but to escape the horrors of her home and the memories of her lost loved ones. She wanted to forget but she could not, and the ribbon of sand moving slowly beneath her feet seemed to cleanse her mind and memory. She was fine as long as she kept moving. When they would stop to camp and build a fire on every other night to rest, she would slip back into despair and loneliness and all of the ribbons of sand , all of the memories of her lost and dead people would come crashing down on her. It would be this way for a long long time and the queen and her children would travel a long long way.

After a week they were at the rocky outcrop and it was as the old story said, a sheer wall that went from out at sea to the mountains inland. Hernia climbed a high sand dune to see if there was a route through the mountains and when she reached the top she saw that the wall ended at a cliff that could not be climbed. It was no wonder that no one had been beyond this point. From her vantage point she could see that the tide was retreating and she also saw where the waves crashed on the point and she wondered how far out the tide would go. She came down from the dune and instructed the boys to gather wood for a fire and they would camp and gather seaweed to eat while they waited on the tide.

It was a beautiful full moon over the water and the sky was clear and bright with more stars than she ever remembered seeing before. Helina walked alone on the beach as the children told stories around the fire. She was trying to delay the memories that encroached on her mind each time that they camped. She wondered how she would feed the four hundred plus children and knew that seaweed was not sufficient. They had not seen any fruit or nuts to eat since leaving East and all were loosing weight from the constant moving on such a minimal diet. The waves made a gentle churning sound and the seam where the water met the land was moving and shimmering with foam and bubbles in the moonlight. She noticed some muscles sticking up from the sand as water receded over them on its way back to the sea. She picked one up and pried it open and without hesitation, sucked the animal juice and all into her mouth and down her throat. It was a pleasure she had never known before and she felt nourished by it straight away. This was her answer for feeding the children. No one in East had ever eaten a muscle before but these were desperate times, and besides it was quite good to the taste. She used her short dress as a cradle and gathered up as many as she could carry back to the camp. Around the fire the children were bewildered by her actions but watched with curiosity. She showed them to eat and a few of the youngest sucked them down without hesitation. The older children, especially the boys were horrified at the idea of eating an animal. Some joined in and ate but many refused. Some vomited afterwards and felt shame and disgust. Before long nearly all were combing the beach for more muscles and they ate until they were full. The children quit telling stories and curled up around the fire and each other and went to sleep. Helina sat on the beach watching the water retreat late into the evening until low tide occurred.

She ran out along side the wall of rock to where it met the sea to discover that the water was only waist deep at the outcrops furthest point. She rushed back calling to the children to awaken and got them to line up one behind the other and instructed them to hold each others waists and to form a chain of people in order to work their way around the wall through the water. The larger children placed the smaller ones on their shoulders and the tallest boys carried the babies. The waves pushed them against the craggy rocks and the sea bottom was slippery rock as well. Helina was first around the point and she climbed a small ledge to supervise the operation and urge the children on. When about half of the line was through the waves became bigger and the water was soon over everyone's heads. Many could not swim and a few lost their grips on the child in front of them and were washed out to sea and drowned. When the front of the line reached the beach it became a group effort to pull the rest of the clinging children to safety. All of the babies were saved but several of the younger girls were lost forever. They lay on the beach to catch their breaths and then began to look for survivors that might wash ashore, but there were none.

The clan was tired from their ordeal but none wanted to rest for long anxious to get away from the wall. The sun was showing its first light over the mountains and everyone just started walking south on the beach without a word from Helina. She was strengthened by the sun's rays, knowing that her father was leading them on to a future of which she couldn't begin to guess. All that she knew was to keep moving, far away from the bitter past and on to another place which could be their new home. She never realized how fortunate the people of East were, with a land so abundant with fruits, nuts and flowers. She thought briefly about the beauty of her home and looked about her and wondered if the world was as barren and unforgiving as where they were. As far as she could see down the beach and when she was on the dune, there was not a living thing, only reddish colored rocky terrain. More than ever the beach would be the provider of sustenance and the road to some place else. She had to follow the sandy trail away from her beloved land to escape the monsters, and the sun would light her path.

Chapter 13

The New Order

The people of East had followed the shore of The Sea for many months, traveling by the light of the sun by day, and sleeping under the stars with the sound of the surf by night. The children did whatever Helina asked of them, for she was the key to their survival. There was no storytelling by the fire in all of these months of travel and the children missed this. Helina had good reason for omitting this tradition for she was about to invoke much change in the culture that had not changed for many millennia. During the long walks by day she had emptied her mind of the grief of the past, which allowed her to contemplate the meaning of all of this change. The paradise that was her home was now a distant fading memory that she would try to extinguish all together in the children. It would be an easy task for the youngest of the children but the older ones were holding on to the memories of the good times they'd had. It is strange, Helina thought, how one tends to remember the good and forget the bad things. She saw this in the older children, as they would also pine away for their parents and lost friends. She would do her best to erase their memories good and bad, for the survival of her people depended on it. Her reasoning was also strengthened by a debt. She knew that they all owed their existence now to the sun, which was a new concept in her culture. Throughout history the debt was to the people, to each other, without the slightest thought to the sun beyond it being a source of warmth and light, much as a campfire would be at night. One would not think of paying homage to a campfire, certainly it was a nice thing to have, but the idea of the sun as a being with a consciousness would have been absurd. All of that was now changed; in fact Helina was contemplating whether or not the moon also was not a being since the rounding of the point at low tide many months before. Was it not the moon that lit the way in that dark hour? Was it the moon that coaxed the water out to sea to make the crossing possible? These were the kind of questions that Helina puzzled over for so long and she was about to make some changes for her people, for her children. They had accepted the eating of animal flesh for the sake of survival and now she would lead them into an acceptance of paying homage to the sun for survival as well.

They came upon a cove at sunset this day and there they saw the first trees that they had seen since leaving their home, small as they were. The campfires had been made of driftwood and dried sea grass but tonight they would use dried branches from these little trees. This would be symbolic for never had they pulled branches from a living tree for any purpose but she felt as though the sun would recognize the act as one of a sacrifice. She instructed the children to build a fire of the living plants and as a diversion there would be story telling on this night. The children were overjoyed at this and went straight forth to collect the wood and built the fire as the sun was setting into the cove of water with a fiery blood red brilliance. She instructed the others to gather muscles and clams, which had for so long supplied their bodies with the water and nutrition to live. There was only about three hundred children left for the elements and disease had taken its toll on this unending journey to what seemed like nowhere.

The children had been buried along the way on the beach with little ceremony, but a cone shaped pile of sand was left to mark the grave so that the sun would know where the child was buried and could come for that child's spirit to take it up with it into eternity.

The fire was not very large but was intense with the popping of new wood and the smell of the smoke was earthier than any could remember before. There is an enchanting quality when a group of like-minded individuals gather about a fire at night to watch the blue, yellow and red flames. The smells and sounds add to the hypnotic and cathartic effect that the fire can induce. The waves were so quiet that they were only an after tone to the crackling flames and the only place of life seemed to be this island of light in an immense universe of darkness and void. Nobody spoke for the longest time, just staring at the flames, nor was anyone thinking except for Helina. She knew the power of the camp fire for setting the tone for story telling as it had a way of opening up the imagination to visualize what was being said. She noticed that this earthy smelling fire had a more powerful effect than ever and she had to fight the drifting of the mind that it evoked. She allowed some time to pass until everyone was peaceful and serene but not yet sleepy. Her timing would be perfect.

Nobody was moving when she slowly and deliberately used her slender young hands to scoop some white sugary sand into a cone shape next to the fire for all to see. She then grasped the sand in her fist and held it over the top of the cone to let it dribble through to make the cone higher with each successive handful. She did this ever so slowly as the sand would roll down the cone yet always getting taller until she stopped when it reached the height of a foot or so. Everyone stared at the cone with the flames reflecting the red hues off of the white crystals that made up the sand. "This, is all we have." she spoke gently and lovingly to the children. "This cone is the symbol of who we are. It has been how we have buried our dead for as long as any one could remember. Why we piled the stones in a cone such as this we knew not. Perhaps they are models of the peaks of our home, which is no longer our home. I am telling you tonight why, even though this image of the cone is all that we have, it is the most important thing in our lives, and have always been the most important thing. It is more important than the people that we love, living and dead. It is more important than the land from whence we came. It is more important than any of the codes or stories of old. It is more important than even the love we have for all things. It is a symbol that you can hold in your heart and feel in your mind. It is the one thing of all things that never changes even through disaster and death. It was always here even before we were here and it will be here long after we are gone. It is silent and unmoving. The wind will blow this little pile of sand away but the entity that this symbol represents will not be blown away by the strongest wind. This, my children, is the sun. The sun is a being of love and hate. He has always been and will always be. He loves us very much for he delivered us from our enemies. And now he will show us to our new home. While you gathered wood I climbed a high dune to see what was on the other side of the cove. The beach makes a turn to the west from here and as I watched the sun set, the shore was leading directly to it. We shall follow the sun to our destiny and ask him no questions. I know not how far we must travel but there also was a lone large black bird flying towards that sunset and I knew that the sun was telling me that the bird knows our home, and when we reach our home, there the bird will be."

The children were looking at Helina with mouths wide yet speechless. This was such new information and most could not grasp the profundity of it all. They loved her deeply and would trust her. Many felt the pain of letting go of the traditions they had been taught but they too were willing to trust her.

She instructed them to eat the clams and muscles but that half of the food must be placed into the fire for the sun, as a token of faith in him. "We must thank our father Sun for saving our lives. You must not question him or talk to him. He tells me what to do in an inner voice that he has placed within me. I am your queen and he is our father. Follow me and you follow him". All of the children agreed without hesitation and did as Helina had instructed. After the meal everyone slept a dreamless sleep so deep that the sun was hot on their faces the next morning before any awoke. The sun was the first thing that the thought about and would dominate their lives from that day forward. They set off walking around the cove and headed west along the shore. It was becoming the hottest day that any one from East had ever known and soon they would be walking towards the sun.

The group walked bare foot in the sand, as they had never worn shoes. Their homeland was such a livable place with its lack of thorny weeds and mild climate, but now the sand was hot to the touch even to the trail toughened feet of these children of nature. They soon found walking unbearable unless they stayed at the waters edge. The landscape was growing more barren with only red rocks and wind blown sand out of the south. At times the huge rocks jutted out into the water, forcing them to go around through the ankle deep hot sand. The sun was beating straight down for the longest time and there was not a shadow in which to hide. The younger children began to cry and lag behind as the older boys carried up the rear urging them on. Helina seemed not to notice the hardship as her thoughts were focused on the path ahead and she even smiled and squinted her eyes shielding them from the blowing sand. There was no water and some of the children began to drink seawater, which made them sick so Helina decided to climb one of the rocks to get a view of what was to the south. She climbed up the hot face of the stone to the peak and was astonished at the sight of a huge expanse of hot, burning sand dunes as far as she could see. Then she saw water, shimmering between some dunes that were perhaps an hour's walk. She looked to the west and saw an opening in the rocks for passage to the water and climbed down to lead the children to it.

The sand was even hotter when they trekked inland but everyone was excited at the prospect of having a drink, so they pushed on. The closer they got to the water the further that it seemed to recede and after two hours of walking, Helina realized that the pond of water was an illusion created by the immense heat. The people were too tired to return to the beach and the sun was at afternoon angles so they curled up in the shadow of a dune and slept for the rest of the day. A few of the children died from the heat and in the evening Helina had a burial for them of course with a cone of sand atop the graves. She gathered the children about and said that the sun had required these two innocent lives as partial payment for the debt and that he would take us out of this life when he chose to, to be with him in eternity. The children were all crying but they were so starved for water that not a tear fell. They made their way at sunset to the beach.

Night brought relief from the scorching heat and a small amount of seaweed was passed around to wet the lips. The eldest boy, whose name was Lithair, could not control his emotions any longer. He stood tall in the middle of the group and looking directly at Helina and shouted, "Your father has killed our beloved sisters, led us into desolation and thirst, and now we will all die from his glorious and shining love. Why do you follow him my queen? His heat burns down on our heads and he bakes the very land wherever we walk to scorch our feet. I say that he is merciless and cruel. I saw what he did to our enemies but why torture us, his beloved? I love you Helina, but I am certain that you are a fool for bringing us to die in this place."

The children showed no emotion at the outburst but Helina walked calmly to his side and kissed his forehead and whispered that she loved him and that he was a sweet and good boy. He fell to his knees and hugged her thighs and begged for forgiveness. "I adore you as we all do, but I do not understand." "Do not worry my love," she reassured, "We all have doubts in the course of the day, every day that we live. That is the beauty of knowing the father. Before him there was nothing to doubt in the world, for our world was simple and death was certain. He gives us the opportunity for life beyond this world, a life with him in the heavens where he dwells. In East our life was beautiful but death was terrible. We had no control over the monsters from the far side of The

Sea. We now control our own destiny, dismal, as it may seem now. When we die now it is the father who takes us to be with him and not an animal that chases us down and rapes us before killing us. Now, nobody eats our babies alive. We may die of thirst or burn in the sand but it is our choice. You are sixteen and a young man now. I count on you to be a leader by my side. You must help me Lithair. You must help the children and trust in the father. We will make it to a new home, and more of us will die, but I need your wisdom and strength to carry me when I have my doubts. We have changed much since the storm but we are still a people, a collective. Walk with me."

Lithair said nothing but stayed on his knees and hugging her tightly. All of the children gathered in a circle around them and fell to their knees in a group hug with Queen Helina standing tall in their midst with the green of the night sea reflecting on her shiny black hair with the sparkle of the stars in her eyes. The warm wind was gentle on their faces and the comforting drone of the surf was in their ears. They were at peace in this moment after yet another day of despair and hardship. "Tomorrow we find water," was the last thing anyone said this night, and it was said by Lithair.

Chapter 14

Survival

    The morning began with a dry mouth and eyes caked with sand. Everyone wanted to bathe in the sea but the salt water would only make the dryness of skin unbearable. There was nothing to eat as not a clam or muscle had been seen for two days. Helina felt strength from the rising sun and she thought that this day would be the most difficult yet and that she had to find water. When everyone was awake they realized that two babies had died in the night. There was hardly a whimper, for death had now become a daily occurrence and they buried them with the proper graves after which Helina spoke a few words of remembrance. There was no time to waste for they were in a race for survival, a slow and tedious race against space and time. They had to cover ground and knew not how much. This was a race where no one knew where the finish was but only knew the reward for the winners, and that reward was life itself. They walked in single file along the beach and the trail was not difficult for the red rocks were gone and didn't have to be circumvented. The dunes disappeared and all there was to their left was flat dry land as far as they could see. It was almost a reflection of the ocean. The wind died completely and there were no waves at all. The only sounds were the sounds of many heavy breaths and the shuffling of feet of all sizes through the sand. The sun grew higher in the sky and was soon directly overhead. The pace began to slow and children began to crawl or just sit down in total exhaustion. They were dying.

Helina did not try to motivate them for she knew that it would be useless to drive on the dying when there was nothing in sight to drive them to. Even if there was a tree or rock to hide under they would still die and most could not go another step. She looked up at the sun that blinded her. Her fair skin was scorched red and peeling as she wept in her mind. What have I done to these children, she thought. There must be a way. She dropped her head in sorrow and as she did her eye caught a flashing reflection in the sand. She bent over and brushed the sand away from the shiny object. It was a sparkling and pointed stone with a sharp edge. She grasped it in her fist and turned it to see the sun reflecting from the many facets. "He has given us the way." she whispered.

Helina walked back to the line of children and looked among them for the dead. She found the girl Souk, who had just expired. Souk was loved by all for her charming smile and gigglish laughter and she even smiled in death as if to say that this situation is rather funny. Helina plunged the stone into Souk's chest and ripped her belly open wide. The children clamored over her, sucking the blood so quickly that not a drop hit the white sand. She went to another dead child and did the same as the next group partook in the life saving liquid, then to another and another. Then Helina herself drank her fill.

They did not bury the drained corpses not having the energy. The wind began to pick up and the group started to walk again. They had started their journey with over four hundred children and now there was less than three hundred. Out of twenty-two babies there now was eight. Helina now knew in her heart that they would make it but at what cost.

She worried because of the girls, only a dozen or so was approaching puberty, but there were many more boys capable of fathering even if they did not yet know it. Once they found a place to take shelter for a time with food and water it would become a priority to couple the eldest children for the sake of their survival as a people. These folk were a ghastly lot, faces covered with dried blood and the look of death in their eyes. They walked automatically in single file never looking behind them or anywhere. Their gazes were fixed on nothing and all minds were blank, slowly moving on in the vast, void of hell. No longer were there thoughts of the past nor of the future, only the present existed but barely. They moved like a many-legged beast with the queen as the eyes. The beast snaked through the sand instinctively in search of water and shade. There was no hurry to find death, so the pace kept slow. This went on for the evening and into the night, through the whole of the next day, which was even hotter, and at sunset they rested. No one had died and everyone was oh so thirsty. The entire group fell to the ground and fell immediately to sleep where not a dream was had. They were the living dead, even in sleep.

Helina awoke before sunrise and walked up the beach for no reason. The moon was nearly full and she pondered whether or not it too was a being. If the sun is a male surely this orb is a female, she thought. The sun is always the same, like a man. The moon changes its face and is hidden and coquettish at times, like a woman. The sun is dominating while the moon is subtle and quiet. The sun compels while the moon coaxes. "I beseech you moon to show me the way in the darkness where we dwell. Show me a way to save my children and I will worship you. You will be our goddess of night while my father sun leads us by day." The moon was almost on the western horizon as the sun was lighting the east. Helina saw ripples in the sand that looked different from the rest of the beach and she walked to it. They were ripples from a dried stream that sometimes makes its way to the sea. She had to decide to keep a western track or follow the dry stream inland to the south. She could see no landmarks or trees in either direction and realized that this would be a life and death choice. She wondered if she should accept the moon's advice and risk angering the sun, or did they work together, or was they enemies? She moaned at the idea of having to decide when a large black bird flew from behind her and turned to the south in the direction of the dried stream to disappear into the twilight. She had her answer and wasted no time in rousing the beaten souls to a final push to try to live. The wind started blowing strong out of the south and into their faces as the sun began its climb. The moon dropped below the horizon and the hardest day of their young lives was under way. She hoped that they would make it.

The route was depressed below the land as one would expect for a dried stream, and they had to walk in this shallow ravine for the sand was soft and deep outside of it. The wind was channeled there to make it blow all the faster, working against the frail bodies and draining their strength. The blowing sand was punishing as it stripped away their flesh little by little. The up hill incline was imperceptible but it was like climbing a steep mountain with each step growing more difficult and each breath harder to take. They suffered terribly this day and each day became worse. After three days of travel and two more bodies sucked dry for moisture, the crusted ground gave way to shallow mud. Soon they were ankle deep and had to make their way on the bank of the still waterless stream. Helina saw something protruding above the barren landscape in the distance and when they got closer she realized that it was a clump of green trees. She didn't have the energy for excitement but felt relief and hope for the first time in days. There might be water to drink, she thought, or at least a bit of shade. "Please! Not another illusion." she said aloud. As the group closed in on the island it grew larger and larger and when they were close enough to distinguish the details they discovered that it was a grouping of several palms of surprising height. They smelled water. A few said water in unison. Some crawled on their knees and bellies the final few yards and one died mere inches away. It was a beautiful and clear spring, very small but deep enough to come up to the chest of a grown man. The bottom was so clearly visible that it almost looked as though it was merely a hole of air. Many tumbled in headfirst while others lay on top of each other drinking. The spring was totally surrounded by laying bodies two and three deep while the water was full of others. The liquid turned a reddish brown color from the dirt and blood on their bodies. Their thirst was quenched and some began to laugh while others cried. They slept in the shade of the trees for the rest of the day, undisturbed by the cruel world outside of that life saving bubble.

The first night in the desert was quiet and cool. There was a light breeze rustling the palms above, and between the fronds, the galaxy was an explosion of twinkling magic. Helina awoke on her back to see the infinite universe like she had never seen it before. Her eyes were reflecting the whole of space with hues of blue and red as she felt in her mind the depth of the emptiness, so full of light and mystery. She wondered at the immensity and she knew at once that she was not a part of this nature. It was distant and cold and foreboding. This space, the night sky was something she had never experienced at home where all of nature was comfortable and had meaning. There were no words to describe this new nature of which she felt certain that she could not know in a million lifetimes. This queen felt tiny like a snail crawling on the earth. Her insignificance made her feelings of anger from her first memory of learning about her immortality resurface, and she was more alone than ever before.

Chapter 15

Anarchy in the West

When the storm suddenly stopped and the wind died early in West, the residences knew that the soldiers would not be returning. Most did not care for they were concerned with their own lusts. The invisible one was in control so it didn't matter any way. No grieving mothers waited by the shore for a glimpse of a ship and no children asked about their father's return. This horrid society cared so little that they began celebrating the early end to the storm. They could return to their atrocities towards one another unimpeded by the minutia of a war. Fires were started early that day and a hunt for fresh animals lasted into the night with the burning of forest. Drunkenness prevailed and a citywide orgy that spread through the streets and houses would not end for days. Bloodletting, rape, incest, bestiality and murder, the burning of people and animals alive, the destruction of a society from within had begun. All was dark in the bright sunlight and the street ran red with the blood of thousands. Night brought hell, with infernos of piles of people amidst laughter and heckling. Limbs flew and heads rolled down streets. The smell of death, burning flesh and boiling blood permeated the air and stones. There was no innocent ones for all were participants, even too the oldest and the youngest.

The Minister of Faith watched the three-day fiasco from his towering red brick structure at the city's center. The crowd grew weary of sex and turned more violent each passing hour and he could hear them getting louder as a huge mob ascended on his residence. There was chanting that the invisible one was a false god, a sham to entice the whole society to invest all of its resources to war. The general and the soldiers were gone and the city guards were not capable of controlling this riot run rampant. The Minister knew he was helpless as he saw many guards stripping off their squirrel hats, which distinguished them from the rest of the population. A revolution was at hand and the attack had begun. The bloodied and filthy rabble was at his door when he leapt from his roof into a fire on the street below. The crowd let out a cheer and went down to the docks to take up the largest ship's mast under construction and dragged it up to the high point which was the Minister's building, forced it through the door and up through the ceiling. They climbed the edifice and finished pulling it up to the top and secured it with leather, twine and pitch. They stripped the bark from the top down and carved the top into a rounded shape with a stone axe. They covered it with oil and blood and placed torches all round the top of the building where it could be seen by all. This was the new god of West, a totem some four stories high atop a five story building, shaped like a penis and glowing shiny red in the smoke filled night sky. This god would reign supreme in west for a long time to come for the people loved their new visible god. He was always present and he was all knowing for thought occurs in the genitals and this erection was the greatest mind of all. The people of West would never have to cut trees and build boats again, but the new god would soon have his own demands. The sun began to rise and the fires burned themselves out with only the forty torches of the new god burned, day and night. Smoke choked the city, as there was no wind to clear the air. All went to sleep for two days without waking and when they did, their new god was there to greet them, so beautiful and so terrible. His name was Baal.

Chapter 16

Mik

The town of Eastland was totally destroyed by recent events and all of the survivors had fled, seeking safety and a new life. The general had perished with his massive army and most of the inhabitants of this once tropical paradise were gone. The animal life had not even returned for such negative forces could still be felt from the atrocities committed by the soldiers before their demise. The killing of the elders, the hunting down and rape of the women and the vicious slaughter of the men left the smell of death in the air. The last child had suffocated, buried in the caves were they could not be extricated from. The landscape had been transformed by the storm and avalanche and this place of eternal beauty would never be the same, and not a soul would ever occupy it again. The love that the peoples of this area had for each other and the land were gone forever and this enclave of nature would become as mundane as any other place in the world.

Amidst the pile of bloodied bodies and body parts of the men that were so brutally murdered by the soldiers of West, was a lone and seriously wounded young man. It was Mik. He laid unconscious for many days beneath the heap of corpses when he came to and dug his way out of the maggots and stench. His wounds had dried but he was weak and at the door of death himself, but he managed after two days to drag himself to the lagoon. He drank the water and ate the grass and flowers by the shore for several weeks, slowly regaining his strength enough to crawl about in search of fruit to eat. He covered himself at night with palm fronds and slept most of the day as well. It would be a long and slow recovery for Mik even though he was young and strong. When he was finally able to walk, he was crippled in one leg and that would stay with him for the rest of his life. His vision was gone in the left eye from where a stone had struck his head during the attack. He was a handsome man, slender and tall and his dignity was not damaged. He retained his stoic countenance and his beauty, though his body was damaged.

Mik walked his land in search of his people and after discovering the killing fields of the women and elders, and through piecing together the story of what had happened to the soldiers, he discovered the lone cave of children whom were missing. He knew that the rest were dead in the other caves for they had been sealed in far too long to survive. There was no sign of Helina's body and he could only guess at what hat transpired after the avalanche that killed the soldiers. He wondered if she escaped with some of the children or were they killed by other soldiers. The huge boats still rocked in the surf and it looked as though there were no survivors from the fleet. He thought long and hard about where the queen might have taken the children if they were alive, and his conclusion was that they headed south.

Mik spent a few days gathering nuts and dried fruit for his journey, fashioned some water containers out of a string of coconuts and headed to the south along the beach in search of his people. Even if no one survived he could not stay in East. It was all death and heartbreak and there was nothing left of his life there. He would follow the same route that the children took and it would take him several months to find them. His heart was full of love and to be alone in this state was painful. He was part of a collective that he must find and even though what he had been through had not killed him, to be separated from his loved ones would mean dying from a broken heart. It was not the way of his people to be alone. That was a living death that he knew would eventually kill him. He had to find someone.

Chapter 17

Island of Learning

The children recovered from their ordeal of the torturous journey with much needed rest in the shade of the palms of their oasis. It wasn't a large clumping of trees so they had to lay close together to keep out of the sun. At night they would spread out and the older children camped on the perimeter under the stars, keeping the youngest ones safe from potential predators of which they had not seen. There were scorpions and fleas but there was no sign of animal life that Helina thought strange as this was the only source of water for as far as one could see. The land was flat all around and sand blew hard during the day. At night the air cooled to a tolerable temperature and before dawn became even chilly. Helina knew that food was the next order of business and on the third day after finding the oasis, she decided to search for some. She remembered seeing how the women of East were captured using a weapon that she had never seen, to slow them down by shooting sticks from a bow with a string. It was very effective, she thought. Trying to imitate the weapon she used trial and error to fashion it out of the existing materials around her but found that palm trees were not suitable for the task. There were loose stones strewn across the landscape, which gave her the idea to try to find an animal to kill by throwing the stone at it. She had seen the soldiers use clubs and stones to kill but that was from a close range. She would have to sneak up on any animal using this method and surprise them with her presence. She picked a stone that fit in her hand nicely and threw it at the ground as hard as she could. The children watched with angst at the violence of such an act. She drew a circle in the sand with a stick and used it for her target. Again and again she threw stones from greater distances until she became quite good at hitting the circle from as far away as she could throw. She soon had the older boys imitating her. And some surpassed her abilities with great ease and seemed to do it as second nature," You four boys will be my great hunters", she told them. They were not sure exactly what that meant.

But it thrilled them to gain their beloved queens attention and admiration.

When the evening came she had the first campfire built since coming to the oasis. The only materials for burning were the dried palm fronds that burnt quickly so the fire was kept very small. She gathered the excited children around under a half moon and gentle desert breeze. A pile of fronds was established nearby and she waited for the magic of the flames to pacify the group. She knew that her timing must be right to let enough quiet time to pass before beginning her story without running out of fuel before she would finish. There was only enough kindling for one fire. Then she began. "You have heard the stories of our people all of your young lives. The tales of love and compassion, tragedies and death. The stories stretch back for thousands of years and we know all of those who came before us. Although the sagas seem to reach back to infinity, they do not. They tell the tale of who we are but they do not tell us where we came from. We have never treated our beloved land with disrespect nor eaten the animals in our world that we adore. This was not always true. The stories that were omitted from before our history begins tell us that we did indeed kill animals. We cut trees as well and yes, we even killed each other. Our ancestors made the decision long ago to become passive and loving to all things in the world. It was after they discovered our home land of East that allowed for this kind of attitude to take root and thrive. East was a paradise which provided for our every need without aggression. Our only enemy were the monsters of Westland. We found a way to survive them and still be true to our ways of living, through a sacrifice of sorts when many of our people died during the great storms. That life has now ended. Our home is gone forever and we are cast out into the cruel world once more as were the ones that live in our pre-history. In order to survive the condition that we now live in, we must adapt their ways. We must be willing to kill to eat. We have eaten our own loved ones after they died by the hand of our father the sun. We live from their deaths. The only way that we can survive is by killing animals. Nothing grows in the desert for us to eat. The sun has led us to this water and now he will feed us if we are willing to be like him. Killers." The last remaining frond burnt out and the fire was a glowing ember with smoke curling up. The wind began to whistle in the trees and a chill fell over the crowd. Nobody said a word and everyone fell to there sides and went to sleep very hungry. Helina turned her back to the children to look at the starry horizon and was ashamed of the great lie that she had told. She'd never lied before. The worst crime in her culture was committed by the queen herself. A terrible lie about her people and history. Perhaps it was true, she thought. There was no way to know this but it seemed to ease her mind and soon she was asleep and dreaming of the hunt.

Helina was awoken before sunrise by laughing children. There was great excitement in the air as the girls surrounded the four oldest boys who were preparing to leave for the hunt. She smiled and stood up in time to see them walking off into the morning desert. Everyone wished them luck in their first day as killers and the queen had mixed emotions about the ambivalence that the children were demonstrating. Never the less she was hungry too and she yelled out to the lads that her blessing was with them.

The older girls grew quite excited at these brave boys going off to kill a beast and Helina saw this straight away. She knew that it was time to educate them in the art of seduction and child bearing. She knew also that the old ways of wanting rather than having would no longer be logical as the numbers of her people were dwindling and the sooner that pregnancies occurred the better. There was not enough room in the oasis for separating the children from the older girls for the purpose of these delicate discussions which inspired her to pursue other constructive adventures. They would need more room, that was certain, and she pondered how they might build a structure to protect them from the heat of the day with such limited materials. They were starving to death slowly and she could not make the children work until they received nourishment, so she spent the day planning in her mind and drawing on the ground an addition to their new home. She felt sure that this island was a temporary place but she dared not risk another trek into the desert without months of building the strength and courage in her loving children. She did not want to loose another but that was sure to happen given the circumstances.

The hunters were in high spirits as the hot sun began to

bake them on their walk about in the desert in search of any living thing that they could throw a rock at. They were chatting and singing and had no clue how to go about looking for animals in this wide open space where one could see to the horizon all around. Finally at noon they happened upon a lone bush that was tall enough to sit under to avoid the unforgiving sun until the late afternoon. They continued their walk to the south and discovered the same dried stream that had led them to the oasis. It would emerge for a time from the desert and disappear beneath the wind blown dirt and sand again. They found that if they kept a due south course, the stream bed would always surface from time to time. They followed this path all of the night and just before sunrise one of the boys slipped in mud just beneath the surface of the earth. They had hoped for another oasis but instead found that the barren desert gave way to a scrub land of low bushes and weeds. The flatness of the landscape turned into gently rolling hills which they walked through until the landscape once again gave way to flat desert. This was a form of an oasis, Lithair thought. Not suitable for humans but perhaps they would find their beast to kill.

They set up camp beneath the biggest bush at the highest point and collected a pile of rocks for weapons and waited the rest of the day, hidden from the fierce sun. Right before sunset they saw a snake, winding its way through the dried stubbles of grass. Lithair grabbed two rocks and ran after it. The snake recoiled to strike back and the boy threw the rock so hard that it took the snakes head off clean in the first shot. Everyone let out a yell of approval and the boys knelt down and consumed the snake on the spot. "This is easy", said the youngest boy Duf. "Well now it's your turn", replied Lithair.

They returned to their camp and waited for the next snake which wasn't long in coming. Duf ran to it with delight, to show that he was capable to the rest. When he caught up to the snake, it coiled to strike just as Duf was ready to let loose with the rock when the snake struck first. Duf's rock fell from his hand as the big snake attached itself to his face. The others ran to help him and one other was bitten in the fight. Lithair picked up a big stone and crushed the snake's head, killing it in an instant. Duf died in a few moments and the other boy died an hour later. This was a terrible blow to the morale of the hunters and a lesson that the two survivors would never forget. There was much to learn about hunting, they thought, but hunger would keep them to the task thereafter.

The boys took the two corpses and skinned them with a sharp stone. They cut off the heads for burial under two little pyramid shaped piles of rocks. The remains were tied with grass around sticks and they headed back to the oasis with snake meat and the meat of their comrades over their shoulders. The feelings they had were mixed with the loss of the other boys but they were coming home with meat. The group could survive a few more days on this amount of food but they would need more, much more food if the children were to survive. They needed another plan.

They were greeted as heroes when they reached the oasis and nobody seemed to notice the missing boys. Everyone ate their share and went fast to sleep. Helina knew what the bulk of the meat had been but said nothing. All that she cared about at this point was the survival of as many as possible at whatever cost. She ate of the meat herself and thought no more of the missing boys.

The next morning Lithair recruited four more boys and were off to the hunt without the fanfare from his previous departure. They had been instructed to bring back more of the sticks that they had used to carry the meat on and any thing else that might be of use. Helina had plans for the remaining children to create sun dried mud bricks on the edge of camp. The work was mundane and difficult during the heat of the day but there was plenty of water to drink and shade to cool down under. The children worked in shifts, hand making the crude gray bricks that were placed in rows to bake in the sun. It helped the group to pass the time and forget about their hunger as long as they were busy. After a few days they had hundreds of dried bricks ready for the construction of low walls that could be covered with the latest palm fronds that had dried and fallen low on the trunks of the trees. They would be held in place with a mud mixture and before long there was three new hovels just outside of the shade of the trees. They were not cool but they were protection from the sun in the day, and the cool desert wind late at night. It was a beginning, Helina thought.

The five hunters made better time to the hunting grounds on this second outing. They rested under the lone bush that was the half way mark and made it to the brush land in only a day and a half. While they were approaching, they saw four hares scrambling to a hole in the ground. They waited , hidden from the hole by some shrubs until one of the hares showed its head which was his last act. Two rocks hit him simultaneously and he fell back into the hole. Lither reached into the hole and grabbed his ears. They ate him on the spot and dropped back into hiding for the next victim. They waited the rest of the afternoon and not another animal appeared.

"This method is far too slow." said one of the boys. Lithair had an idea. The boys set a series of snares all around the hole by bending branches from the brush and held them in place with twine fashioned from the dried grass forming a circle. They did not use bait and the snares were crude but they compensated for this by quantity. They set fifteen in all and a hare would have to walk or hop through them just to get wherever hares went. The traps would do nothing more than hold the animal until they returned. When the traps were finished being set, they walked to the far side of the hilly area, killing snakes all the way for snakes were abundant. Lithair instructed the rest to not get close to the snakes and to try and kill them from a distance. The strategy worked and the boys became quite good at killing something with a rock from far away. They were proud to have more snakes than they could carry home and made their way to the oasis with bundles of sticks and meat.

Helina separated the older girls from the children and took them into one of the hovels for a private discussion on the finer points of luring a mate. She told them that although the traditional methods of courtship were preferred, there was no longer the luxury of waiting and playfulness. "We are in a fight for the survival of our people. There have been many deaths since we left our home and now there is no time to waste. You all must do your best to become pregnant and to have as many babies as you can. Do not be selective about your mate and receive any advances toward you with acceptance and aggression. There are no husbands now, only partners for conception. You must lure the older boys with seduction and lies if needed. Let them think that you love them if that is the only way. Do not become attached to them for it is important for you to conceive from many different partners. I ask you my sisters, to heed my words and do as your loving queen commands you to do." This was the first time that Helina had commanded. Her way had been one of requests and gentle persuasion. This new style of command pleased her just for the quickness and finality of her words. The girls did not question her desires and this would bolster her confidence in leadership from this time forward. It made her think about any future disputes which might require more than her words to enforce her laws. She knew that she would someday require force to control her people and she began to plot for this inevitability.

After the intimate talk with the future mothers of her new society, Helina initiated another phase of hovel building. This time the children would work through the long days and all night long as well, to build three new edifices that were much larger than the first two. The hunters arrived with the meat and everyone ate enough to keep their strength up to perform the work. She allowed the hunters to rest for a few hours and then sent them out with four additional children to help carry loads of sticks and meat. The hunts and the building construction continued non stop for several weeks there after and five children died from the heat and malnutrition. They were of course eaten and the heads buried after even the brains were devoured for nothing was wasted in this unforgiving land. After the younger hunters became proficient at killing snakes and hares, Helina recruited Lithair to be in charge of a police apparatus to keep the children working and to punish the disagreeable. The harshest penalty, death by stoning, was reserved for outright defiance while lesser crimes such as laziness, or failing to mate would carry the consequence of having to sit in the sun all day without water. If the father sun was forgiving, the child would survive and be welcomed back into the group. If the child perished, its remains would be eaten and the skull would be burned instead of having the proper burial with the pyramid of stones, for the sun would not welcome that person into his realm of eternity in the sky.

There would only be a few transgressors of the laws for the punishments were severe and no one forgot the sight of the agony of someone baking to death. They had experience this from the long journey from East, and that was etched in their memories.

When the walls of the first of the large hovels were finished, a roof was installed using the sticks and branches as support, then covering them with dried fronds. The building was spacious and cooler than the smaller ones as there were doors on each end to allow for a breeze. It could sleep twenty and in the day provide shade for more. The skins of the hares and snakes were fashioned into clothing and beds, replacing the long since worn out traditional clothes made from a woven grass. The animal skins were more durable and everyone seemed to enjoy how the fur felt on the skin. Animal bones were used as tools for everything from sewing to cooking and Lither was working on a new weapon as instructed by the queen, using bone fragments shaped and sharpened to be used as arrow heads on the tips of the straightest of the sticks. Some of the branches were suitable for a bow and the string was strips of leather that was twisted and wetted. On the far side of the camp was the target range where all of the boys would practice shooting arrows into fronds supported by sticks for targets. The girls would watch during their breaks from work and cheer for the great hunters which inspired the boys to compete. There was amorous behavior between many of the boys and girls and Helina felt that she had better pair them off with ones whom they showed little interest in to avoid the complications of petty love affairs. She called to Lithair and instructed him to mate with the girl Sabal. He had no objections for Sabal was lovely and very well developed physically. Sabal had her eye on another boy and seemed completely enamored with him. She didn't resist when Lithair took her by the wrist to take her to bed but she glanced back at her favorite and shed a tear as she went to one of the small hovels to do her duty. This routine would be repeated with the oldest children and soon there were seven pregnancies. Nobody was certain whom fathered whom but that was not important. There was no love or love making involved as was Helina's plan. Her goal was to at least stabilize the population and with luck, it would grow.

Lithair's army of police/hunters grew to include twenty of the largest boys. They would rotate troops between the hunt and the policing of the population, sending fifteen to the hunt for not much police work was needed in camp. Everyone was well behaved as the queen was ever present and the sun was a constant reminder of the punishment. It was still a happy group and everyone was being well fed and clothed with water and shelter. Helina knew that they would out grow this oasis if the population increased and she began to worry about the spring as the water level had dropped slightly in the past few weeks. She didn't know if it would come back to the original level or continue to drop slowly, but she had to think far in advance for the survival of her people. On this morning's hunt she instructed the boys to push further into the desert to see what was beyond the low hill scrub land. There was dried meat stored to last for a time so they could take a longer trip to explore. Lithair agreed with her and said that the hares were thinning out and he didn't know how long it would be before they hunted the place clean. They had not seen a snake in a month and he took that as a sign as well. "We will take enough water to push into the desert for one week. If we find nothing we will take a larger group on the next trip and take water for three weeks. We will find another hunting ground my queen but it may take time".

The boys filled water bags made from the skins of hares and their bows and arrows. As they departed Helina said a prayer to the sister goddess, the moon. "If you have any influence on our father sun my dear sister, please beseech him to let his light shine dim for this hunt. These boys are our food and our future. They hold the seed of our next generation. They are a good and handsome lot you must agree. Watch over them at night and guide them with your golden glow to our true home. We cannot stay in this oasis forever for it is our life boat but it is beginning to sink. I trust in you for the night of light and reason. Thank you my sweet sister". Helina turned around to see the children working on the bricks. "There will be no more building my children. Today we sing and laugh".

When the night had come and the children were asleep, Helina walked far away from the camp into the cool dry desert. The wind was gentle on her fair face and twisted her long black hair around her neck. The brilliance of the night sky in this flat and featureless landscape engulfed her in a reverie of boundless wandering. There was no moon and the stars looked as though she could touch them. She thought of the boys on the hunt and of the children she had lost. She thought of the sun and wondered at his strange ways of teaching and punishing. She thought of her home and its beauty and serenity. She thought about the people of that home who were all gone now and it all seemed like a dream. There had been no time until now to think of the past. She was saddened by it all and she fought to rid her mind of the past but she could not. A fire burned deep within her heart that she could not extinguish. She had developed the hatred that began in the little cave on the peak during the storm and it grew each day, each step down the beach. It grew with the death of every child. The general was killed and that gave her great pleasure and for a moment that fire grew dimmer. She hated the monsters from West with all of her soul and she knew that someday she would kill every last one of them. She was no longer the innocent and witty girl of what seemed like a lifetime ago. She was a different person and she hated that most of all. That girl died on a mountain and this new woman was now being born in a desert. Her mind was matured and her heart was now frozen and as hard as a stone. She then thought about Mik. It was a fleeting thought of his face. She was fond of him before and had things been different, he might have made a good companion. He was the first and only crush she'd had as a young girl. It was one of those childish fantasies that go away after a time. Why him now? It's funny how the mind works in the desert at night. One drifts like a boat with no rudder and the mind flows with the tides of the cosmos. She breathed a quiet laugh and turned to walk back to the oasis. It took her a long while to return as her pace was slow and at times she would stop and think of nothing. When she arrived to her bed she collapsed into a deep and dreamless sleep until dawn.

Helina awoke to a great clamor of yelling children and running feet. The sun was on her face and she could not see for a moment and the children where around her all talking at once. "A man!" cried a little voice. She sprang up from her bed as the children dragged her half asleep into the desert where a group of other children were gathered. Helina walked as the group opened up to reveal an outstretched figure in the sand. He was face down and his ragged clothing was the customary dress of woven grass from Eastland. "Turn him over!", she yelled. "Slowly". As he was pulled by an arm to a face up position she saw that the man was dead. He had grown stiff but had not been dead for long. She listened for a heart beat and there was none. "Get some water", she said softly. He was covered with dirt and sand and there was dried blood around his mouth. The queen dripped water on his face to clear away the dirt and was astonished to see that it was Mik. She stood up and looked around and realized that she had been standing not twenty feet from this spot the night before. "Mik, you were here with me last night",she said so softly that no one heard. She could not believe that Mik was here. She had assumed that he was dead. Her mind had trouble comprehending what had happened. She and Mik were together as he laid dying. He was so weak the night before that he could not call out to her. He had crawled on his belly the final day of his trek. He was making his way to the oasis and you could see by his trail that he made a detour to where Helina had walked out into the desert. Helina was crushed. Had he gone for the water he might have lived. Instead, he came to me and I did not see him. I felt him and his mind touched mine as he lay dying. Had I looked around and seen him I could have saved him. She realized at that moment that she loved him dearly. The young girl's crush from long ago welled up in her heart like a shooting star. She was in love with a dead man. She ran back to her bed crying uncontrollably while covering her face with her hands. She did not want the others to see her cry but they knew. She would stay in her bed for two days in a fetal position, sobbing like a heart broken widow.

When her sorrow subsided enough to drag herself back into the world Helina went straight away to where Mik had been on the ground. The children had placed him on a bed of fronds not knowing what else to do. They watched over his body like angels to keep away flies and scorpions. She admired the children for this and kissed them on the head. "Mik shall have a burial like non before him", she told the children. "Dig a large hole next to his body as deep as you can. We will honor him in death as he honored us by coming to find us. The father sun sent him to us and now we send him to the father. His coming here is a sign for us to move on into the desert in search of a home. This oasis has saved our life and gave us time to gain strength to go on. Remove the bricks from the hovels and pile them up near the hole that you dig. Mik will never be forgotten and we will build a stairway to the sun for him to climb to meet his father." The children formed a line to pass the gray bricks from the hovels to the burial site. They worked without stopping for two days and the hovels were gone.

The hunters had been gone a week and were now seen returning on the horizon. Helina walked to greet them and saw that they had a deer carried on a stick and some flowers.

"We have found another oasis that is much bigger. There is a spring on the edge of a forest of small trees a two days walk past the hilly scrubland. We did not go far into the forest and saw deer and hare and birds. There is green grass and many small trees for shelter and fire wood. I think, my queen that we can make a better life there." Lithair described the place in detail for Helina who said with a low voice, "In two days, we move". She led the boys back to the burial site and everyone including Helina helped to build a pyramid of steps over the buried body of Mik. They took great care to line up the crude bricks as straight as possible and filled in the cracks with mud. They finished the building on a sunrise and it was beautiful as the morning light turned the mud bricks a slate blue color. They gathered up all of the sticks and built a fire at the base and Helina placed the deer on the pyre to burn as a sacrifice of faith. The best food that they had seen since leaving their home. "Mik was not an eater of animals just as we were not. We give him this meat now for strength to finish his journey into the sky". Everyone was hungry but no one complained and many cried for Mik. The little girl Meesha picked up the flowers and placed them on the first step of the pyramid, "Something sweet for you to smell on your journey Mik", she said with the sweetest and softest voice. " Now we must leave", said Helina. The children gathered up water and their meager belongings and headed out into the desert. After a ways they all stopped to turn around and look at the smoke rising up from the pyramid. The sun cast a long shadow of it to the left that covered the oasis that had saved their lives. They took comfort that the father would spare them suffering this day and the desert didn't seem as hot as it felt before. Helina knew that the desert had not changed but her children did. They were happy for the first time and all seemed of a collective once more. "This island taught us all something about the desert, about our father, and most of all about ourselves", she whispered.

Chapter 18

A Dark People

The forty torches burned with a putrid smoke as the original wooden ones were replaced with large fat burning flames. There was a steady supply of the fat of people being hauled up to the top of the red brick edifice. The phallus glistened with oil and blood as it towered over the city of West. It was mid day and the sky was dark with smoke. The entire population of this wretched city had all become equals, slaves and guards alike. Everyone in the street below the monument carried torches in a ceremony that was centered on the enormous wooden penis. A screaming and naked virgin was dragged to the top by a succession of ladders. Her hands were tied with long strands of leather that dark robed men at the top pulled her up by, scraping her back side on the splintered wood and sharp red bricks. She kicked her legs and bit at the leather in an attempt to escape as everyone laughed and screamed at her. Once on top of the building, two black robed men who stood on top of the penis were thrown the leather ropes to pull her up the side to the top. They tied her down belly up and as her long red hair flailed in the smoke and wind the men drove a wooden spike into her heart until it penetrated her spine and stuck into the wooden head. They cut loose her hands to watch her struggle and scream with blood squirting straight up in the air to mimic ejaculation. She fell limp and her blood poured down the sides. Oil was poured over her body and the blood and oil ran down the height of the erection. The women of West took turns masturbating against the phallus in a group of unending procession. They wailed with delight under the light of the torches in knee deep blood that poured off the edge of the roof and the people below would drink of this falling mixture of body fluids and filth. The process was repeated until ten virgins were devoured in this manner each day at mid day. It was difficult to find so many virgins in West so the criteria for proving the virginity was not stringent. They had started a farm of virgins who were closely guarded but during the nightly orgies they sometimes would be taken out of their cages and defiled. This new religion was still in its infancy and the people of West had not yet worked out all of the kinks, but time would develop it into a fine and new faith based on Baal.

The people were thrilled with their new religion for it meant no more ship building. This new god was the god of leisure and pleasure. They still hunted for a time but they found that eating each other was much easier. The old and the very young would be the staple of food supply and they could bring eating into their religion by making every meal a human sacrifice to Baal. The virgins would not be eaten but would remain staked to the top of Baal in a pile of bloodless flesh that grew each day creating a fine bulbous and leathery head. The birds would pick out the bones and leave a smooth corpse behind in an ever growing mass of drying skin with fresh dripping bodies on top.

This culture had slipped into total and complete decay and decadence. Although it had always been an evil city, West was now without goals or faith. Baal was an excuse to unleash the darkest side of these people and they would continue their slide into the abyss of blackness and torment until the city was literally a hell on earth. The nightly orgies diminished for the people lost interest in each other. The focus of the community became masturbating with Baal, or alone on a street corner. It was an entire culture turning inward on itself on every level. No longer did they have interests in building or waging war. No longer did they have a passion for sex with each other. No longer did they have the external invisible god of the desert. They only had themselves in the purest form. Their vision grew dim for eyes were no longer needed. Disease ran rampant for the habits of filth and the loss of interest in food weakened their bodies and they became thin. Fires would burn in the city out of control as if it were in a perpetual natural disaster. Sick people ejaculating in death with tongues thrashing and eyes bulging, vomiting blood and drinking ones own urine for pleasure. They declined into being shit eaters and mud layers and even the pigs were ashamed of them. They were the scum of the earth and the shame of beasts, and their city crumbled around them.

Chapter 19

The Hawk

The children of East made their way happily through the desert to the south once more and for the first time, optimism and joy was felt by all in a collective spirit that was led by Helina. Lithair was by her side as the merry band came to the hilly scrubland and made camp for the evening of the second day. He was her constant companion now and her orders were directed to him and he passed them down to his deputies. It was a kind, but strict form of government meant for the good of the people and the survival of the collective. Several girls were beginning to show from pregnancy and they were granted every privilege from extra food rations to a light work load. This was part of the queen's plan to inspire more conceptions and to protect the unborn, for they were the future. The group had become adapted to the desert heat and could travel with ease, especially now that they carried a supply of water. They were a thin lot from existing on hare and snake for so long but they were alive and full of vitality. These children of the beach had become desert nomads. They carried with them the spirit of their culture as for the love that they held for one another, and although they had lost some of their innocence, the one thing that kept them motivated was hope. Hope for a return to the way of life that they had lost since their home was destroyed. Helina had a different perspective. Her hope was for a new society altogether, with her in control of her people. Her vanity was growing with the taste of power that she had experienced and she was certain that she knew what was best for her people.

Only the hunters had been to the hilly scrubland before so the children were excited to see any variation in the flat desert landscape. Even the queen had not been there and it made her think of Mik, who loved to go to the mountains of the north of Westland to pick mushrooms once a year. Mik was a lover of hilly landscapes and as a young child would slip off alone from the group to the nearby blue hills to walk and explore. This inspired Helina to order that a fire be built on the high spot for a time of story telling. Lithair thought that it was a good idea to keep any snakes away that were not already hunted and suggested that everyone stay as close to the fire as was comfortable. There was plenty of sticks to burn and a sizable fire was blazing in short order with eager faces aglow round about it. Helina was quiet for a time as was the usual first step in story telling and she looked at the circle of happy faces reflecting the flames. It was the first time that she noticed how dark the children's skin had become from the desert sun, with their white eyes and teeth glowing out of the dark. A bank of clouds rolled in and that was the first time that they had seen moisture in the air since arriving in this barren and dry land. As Helina began her story about Mik, the crowd was transported to their home land for a time. The swirling fire was like a time machine that took everyone back before the catastrophe had changed their lives so. The story was about Mik's free spirit and she compared him to the big black bird that led them to the oasis. He was observant of the signs in nature that foretold of changing weather and even when there were no signs, his intuition about the future was always correct for his insight was keen. The children found this all very interesting but when Helina's story slowly became about how lovely Mik's eyes and lips were, or how strong and handsome he was, the group started drifting and each was thinking their own thoughts about their life in West. The boy that they had a crush on or the time a friend was stuck up a tall tree and they had to run for an elder to help figure out the dilemma. Everyone was reminiscing and became saddened, thinking about their parents or friends that were lost. The children nudged closer to one another for comfort and some wept quietly. Helina's words seemed to fade from their ears as they thought of their own grief on this hill by the fire in the dark night. She spoke of Mik as being a big black bird flying in the sky with the sun, watching over and guiding them. She thought of what it might have been like to have kissed his lips. Her heart was softened by love for a short time, an imaginary love that in some ways was more real to her than any she'd known. Mik's spirit would balance her temperament from this time on, and she was pleased with this. She knew that her heart had grown cold and bitter and this bird slowly soaring above her in her mind lifted her hopes and dreams of life and love. She had hidden that part of her away in the same dark recess from whence came the feelings of hate and anger. The black bird would always remind her of that part of her self that she liked. He would be the inner strength for her when determined hatred would not carry her through trying times. Helina smiled and cried with the children on this first and only night that would be the final wake for their lost culture and loved ones. She didn't know how her story turned into this emotional moment, for she wanted to keep the children focused on the future. Perhaps it was the hills and the fire, or perhaps it was the leaving of the oasis. At that moment she heard a solitary hawk's single cry high above them, and she knew that it was Mik.

Chapter 20

The Woods

The night spent at the hilly scrubland was a spiritual catharsis and a physical rejuvenation. The clouds in the air came to rest on the earth in the morning and there was a beautiful fog causing water droplets to collect on the branches and the noses of the children who licked them repeatedly. The fire was smoldering and had the smell of the damp leaves of autumn which would soon disappear when the desert sun cooked away all trace of moisture. It would be hot very soon and the group was making tracks to the south on the next leg of the trek. Everyone was quiet and smiling yet full of energy. Helina's face had a rosy tint and her dark eyes were clear. She had a grin so wide that she covered her face with a cloth for fear of looking silly. She thought about the hawk's cry all day and was genuinely happy and had to refrain from speaking for fear that it would turn into giggling. She felt younger than her twenty years and walked near the young girls to hear their frivolous conversations. The pace of the walk was brisk and there would be no rest until the hottest part of the day when they would set up small tents with sticks and fronds for shade and pass around a skin of water. They napped for some time and being well rested, Helina decided to travel on through the night under a bright moon. The trail of the creek bed came and went but was easy to follow. When their feet began to sink in mud their hearts rose with excitement about seeing the land of many small trees as described by the hunters. At sunrise they could finally see the little forest come into view and some of the children ran to the trees to embrace and climb them. They acted as though they were seeing a long lost friend. When one has not seen one for a long time, trees are a joy to behold and in a way it is like coming home. The dried stream bed gave way to water which led to a large pond surrounded by green grass with willows and small oaks. The forest was made up almost entirely of the small oaks. The climate was still arid and the gentle rolling landscape of dried grass and short trees would not have qualified as a wooded area in the north, but in this desert it was certainly a lush and livable place that most certainly harbored animals. They found an outcropping of rock near the water's edge. A clearing of green grass with the rock wall on one side and water on the other with willows at each end of the camp site. The place seemed perfect for protection from the wind at night and the blazing sun in the day. The air was cooler by the water's edge and the children sat in the green grass and soaked their tired feet in the pond. They watched bugs on the surface and saw small fish eating them. There were birds singing in the trees and the sound of the wind blowing through the willows made the place seem alive.

The girls set up camp to be as comfortable as possible while the hunters went in search of food. First they went about the woods nearby and gathered dead branches and looked for edible roots. The ground was soft under the green grass by the pond and they shoved the longer branches into the earth to form a series of circles. They bent the branches over to meet in the center and tied them off to create a dome shaped skeleton for smaller branches to be woven through horizontally. The process was repeated with still smaller sticks vertically and the domes were skinned with willow branches and leaves. They used mud from the pond to fill in the cracks and left small openings for entry. Helina was amazed at the inventiveness and resourcefulness of the girls and she let them all know what good work they had done. The children needed their queen's approval from time to time and Helina knew that it was essential for creating unity in the group. She was not generous with her pandering but was timely and genuine and the children knew this. It was special to be singled out for good work but it was not their motive for they were a collective still in every sense of the word.

The hunters goal was to seek out a deer. They had only killed one and they were not sure exactly how to go about it but they were certain that it would take a bow and arrow. They had become good at stalking the hares of the scrubland and took this approach for the deer. They walked quietly and softly through the woods but had trouble with stepping on dried twigs and branches which made snapping noises. They agreed that a smaller group would make less noise, so Lithair and one other boy named Hew, went alone and left the rest to sit in a clearing to make more arrows. They used a trick they had learned from hare hunting of looking for droppings of feces from the deer. If it was wet and fresh it meant that they might be close to one. They soon sighted droppings in a small clearing and decided to sit in a thicket nearby to see if one showed up, and soon one did. It was a beautiful buck with small antlers and a white mane. They were in awe of the creature and watched it lovingly without making a noise. They watched him for a long time as their hearts were beating out of their chests with excitement. The buck finally smelled them and darted away through the woods without the boys even shooting one arrow. It had never occurred to them to kill him. They felt stupid having missed such a fine meal for the group but the old ways of walking softly on the earth overcame even their hunger. They were not ashamed and they decided to never tell a soul what had happened. Lithair was a lover of the animals and was a hunter for survival only. He would think of the beautiful buck in that clearing for a long time to come and would sometimes sketch him in the dirt with a stick to refresh his memory.

The two great hunters ran back to meet up with the rest who were waiting in the clearing to see them in the process of stoning to death a doe. There was a single arrow in her head and the group had her on the ground still kicking. One of the boys took a large rock and smashed her skull to finish the job as she struggled for her life. Lithair was horrified at the violence and became disgusted when a few of the hunters laughed at her pain and demise. He held those feelings to himself but did not offer congratulations either. The doe was tied to a branch by the legs and carried back to camp in a victory parade of whistling and dancing. A trail of blood followed them the whole way but nobody paid attention to that. The collective was resourceful at the site of the meal and the girls built a fire to roast the doe over. Cooking the animal was suggested after someone remembered how good the smell of burning deer was in the sacrifice to Mik. At meal time everyone ate a portion except Lithair who feighned a stomach ache and went to his bed early. He was sickened by the smell of the burnt flesh and he never forgot the fear and helplessness in the animals face before receiving the final blow to the head. He felt sorry for her and he would never eat deer meat. As he fell asleep he had blood in his nostrils from the smell of the kill in camp.

Something woke Helina in the middle of the night but she didn't know what it was. Everything was silent and dark, the camp fire was smoldering and there was a heavy fog in the air. She heard the unmistakable sound of a growling dog so close that she could smell its breath. She could see nothing in the fog shrouded dark of night and the hair stood up on the back of her neck. She heard two or three animals growl at the same time and she screamed out of a primordial fear of suddenly becoming prey. Everyone jumped awake and Lithair and a few other boys instinctively grabbed a weapon. A pack of wild dogs was running through the camp in the next instant. They attacked the smallest children and started dragging them off into the dark. Everyone found themselves in a fight for their lives as the dogs kept coming in numbers too numerous to count. The fog was so thick that they were invisible until their jaws were around a neck or limb. A few boys had the presence of mind to let loose a volley of arrows, killing three dogs before they were overwhelmed by the onslaught. Children were dragged off into the forest and screams could be heard as they died a terrible death. Helina was frantic but was unable to help them as everyone was surrounded, kicking and gouging at the animals until suddenly the pack ran off to wherever they came from. The survivors were screaming and ran to Helina. The boys made a valiant circle around the group and there they sat the rest of the night, hunters with bows stretched and aiming into the fog. There was blood everywhere as Helina took a count to discover that the dogs had made off with at least ten of the smallest children. There were many wounded including Helina who had a chunk of her wrist bitten off. They decided to get into the water to wash off the wounds and to wait out the night, shivering in fear. Lithair thought about the doe that was killed and he knew exactly how the animal felt just before her death.

The fog was heavy the rest of the night and on into mid morning. Helina and two of the boys decided to venture out from the protection of the group to see if there was any sign of the missing children. They carried big sticks that they held in front of them to prod their way through the fog and made a quick search of the perimeter. The only signs were blood splattered all around the brush and willow trees but there was no trace of survivors. Her heart sunk at the realization of this yet another terrible tragedy and she promised herself that the dogs would never do this again. When they returned the fog started to thin and she had the boys build a quick fire. "We must keep a fire burning all night or when there is fog from now on", she commanded. She instructed the children to build a fence on each side of the camp. The water and the rock wall would protect the front and rear. The fence was made by piling up stones with broken branches and sticks facing outward higher than a dog could jump. A narrow entry was left with an additional fence placed further out to where the animals would have to make a turn before entering the camp. It created a bottle neck to slow them down and to focus the pack into a single file attack where the hunters could manage a defense. Helina's anger grew and her hatred of the beasts enflamed revenge in her heart and she could think of nothing else. She instructed the hunters to train every child in the bow and arrow and the art of killing and self defense. Piles of fire wood were stored within the camp and more shelters were ordered built. She organized a hunt for the children and the dogs with herself in the lead. She left Lithair in charge of the camp with half of the boys and set out in search of where the dogs might spend their days.

The woods covered a large area that took a full days travel to cross and at the far end was the continued expanse of open desert. It was to dangerous to travel at night so they set up camp in the open desert until dawn to make the return trip. They saw neither a dog or a child. She decided that hunting the dogs was an improbable task and that splitting up the group for so long was unwise. It would be better to have a fortified camp, never allow the youngest children to venture out and to keep the hunters close enough to allow their return before dark. She knew the dogs would return but after several nights there was no sign of them. They could not live in this grip of fear, the same way that her people had lived for thousands of years, awaiting the monsters from the west. Just as she had decided to destroy the Westlanders, the dogs would suffer the same fate. When hatred took over her mind, no enemy would be safe. The flame of revenge in her was only diminished by the act of killing the object of that revenge. The west would have to wait but the dogs were in her reach.

A plan was created to lure the pack to the camp in the form of baiting. She had the hunters kill several deer that were piled up inside the camp by the rock wall. She remembered how the sun had saved the children from the soldiers of West in the form of a landslide. He had taught her a lesson of survival on that day and she was just now realizing that. She could not create a landslide of
rocks, but if she could lure the animals into a small space,

she could create an onslaught of arrows. The hunters fashioned many more bows and began intensive training for every child who had strength to draw one, and those who didn't were busy making new arrows.

They built another barricade of tree limbs and positioned themselves between it and the edge of the pond. Whenever the dogs attacked, they would be forced to enter the camp through the narrow opening in the main barricade after being slowed by the turn. They would then be trapped between the two barricades and the rock wall with the pile of rotting deer meat. Helina hoped that the pack would choose the deer over the people but there was no way of knowing that for sure. As a last line of defense, the group would rush into the water if the dogs began to overwhelm them. The pond was about neck deep to an adult in the middle where the boys had lashed together several small logs to create an island that was anchored with a large stone. They would place the smallest of the children on the island with a few girls to care for them and make sure that they did not fall into the water and drown.

As evening approached, a fog began to waft its way into camp and progressively became thicker. Soon the dogs were heard howling in the distance as they could smell the meat. Helina had everyone in their positions with a row of eighty archers on the front line behind the second barricade. The younger boys and girls stood behind them with piles of arrows to distribute as needed. Lithair was on a big rock overlooking the action with his bow readied while Helina stood atop another rock by the pond with her bow. She hoped that the fog would not be as thick as the last attack, and that she could see all of the action. Her last order before the attack was for the camp's fire to be extinguished.

Everyone was silent and could hear the dogs approaching in what sounded like a huge pack. There was a half moon filtering through the thickening fog that cast an eerie glow, and their visibility was good enough to see the whole camp. Helina said an audible thank you to her sister moon as the first dog became visible just outside the entrance to camp.

The pack came growling and grunting through the entrance in twos and threes, leaping over one another while negotiating the turn. The outer barrier slowed them down and they piled up to wait their turns to gain entrance to the camp. Many tried to scale the barricade and a few made it over by climbing on top of the frenzied pack. Helina could not see much beyond the barrier but there were dogs as far as she could. The archers let loose the arrows in rapid succession as the dogs went for the deer. Many were killed and injured straight away and fell to the ground adding to the confusion. Dogs were tearing at the meat from all sides and began to bite each other. The camp was over run with the animals and many charged the second barricade. Not a child flinched in the face of the jaws of death and volley after volley of arrows flew into the eyes, heads and chests of the dogs. They kept coming through the entrance with no end of the pack in sight. The dead and dying dogs provided a staircase over the second barricade and the archers kept to the task. Helina ordered a retreat to the water as the brave warriors began to fall under the wave of teeth and fur. Most of the children made it to waist deep water and continued to shoot into the beasts. Several dogs followed them but were easy targets as they swam. A dozen archers made their way to the log island and were shooting over the heads of the front line to slow the dogs progress even more. Helina heard a scream and saw a girl trapped on the shore who was being eaten alive by the pack just below the rock that Lithair was standing on. He had his bow and arrow pulled back and was aiming at the child devouring dogs but froze in position and did nothing. Helina was shouting and shooting her arrows as fast as she could but there were too many of the beasts and the girl succumbed quickly. The queens anger flared and she became dizzy with disgust and revenge. She pulled her bowstring as hard as she could and let loose with a single shot to the heart of Lithair. He fell dead to the ground and the dogs consumed him in seconds.

Helina looked to the entrance and saw that there were no more dogs coming in. This pack was huge but it was not endless. Arrows flew from the water as dog fell upon dog. Many ignored the children in favor of the pile of meat and some were eating dead dogs. Some were swimming to the archers who dropped their bows to try and drown them in a hand to mouth combat to the death. Helina never slowed in her stream of arrows as two children passed them up to her from the water behind the rock. The tide of the battle was turning and the sound of growls and barks gave way to whimpers and yelps. The arrows were still coming when as if a whistle blew, the pack ran for the entrance for their lives as still more fell in retreat. They ran off into the fog not to be seen for quite some time. Dogs gasped last breaths and choked on their own blood as the group of mighty warriors let out a collective scream of victory. Helina stood atop the rock with her bow raised above her head and was as still as a stone for a few moments. The children yelled her name again and again. The fog cleared and the moon was above her head, and everyone knew that Queen Helina was truly the daughter of the sun and the sister to the moon and the lover of the hawk.

Helina spoke only briefly for there were many wounded. "We are the masters of these woods. No creature will be against us for we are a collective. Lithair died a coward. Bury him with the dogs".

Only four archers and one sister had died in the battle of the dogs. Many more had bites but they would heal. Lithair was not in the body count and his name would never be mentioned again. The children went about killing the wounded dogs with sticks and stones and tended to the injured archers. They spent the whole night pulling the dead animals out of the camp and threw them into a ravine far away. Lithair's remains were tossed into the pit last, and some of the children spit on him. They walked home in the dark woods unafraid.

Helina saw that her victory over the dogs was the impetus that she needed to dispel any doubts that the children might have harbored secretly about her power, or the change in their culture. The arrow through the heart of Lithair was a finishing blow to what had been. There was now no more history but hers. This clan was making its own history, independent of the mythology of the people of East. Their ancestors were as dead as the dogs and as forgotten as Lithair. Her new order had come to fruition and the children would follow her anywhere. She would have their complete obedience and their unshakable admiration. She was approaching the status of a goddess to them and in her own mind, she wondered if it were not true. She decided that her people needed a new name, an identity that they would embrace and one that would strengthen the bonds of the collective. Helina would create a powerful nation from this tattered band of nomad children. They would grow in number and courage. They were now the great warriors of the woods and her goal was to make them the warriors of the world. Never again would they walk silently to the slaughter or hide in caves from the monsters. They would walk tall on the earth with all other creatures beneath their feet. The desert had been their death and the woods was now there rebirth. Helina and the children had been through a great change together in their quest for survival and a new home. The hearts and souls of even the youngest were altered forever by their journey towards their destiny, overcoming fear and physical suffering. They had found new light in the sun and new courage in the moon, and they had found new direction in the hawk. Their queen was the mediator between them and their new gods. She and she alone would name them, and from this day forward they would call themselves the Helinites. They would become known as the stalkers of prey and the biters of dogs. The killers of killers and the hell of the night, and no beast would be safe from their power and resolve.

The Helinites honored their queen in the form of a temple of stone and logs on the highest hill in the center of the woods. Each new moon they would sacrifice a deer by tying it to a stake and shooting it in the heart with a single arrow in her honor. Each full moon they used the temple to honor the sister moon with a sacrifice of flowers, and every sunrise the new nation would greet the father sun from the temple as he rose in the east. The hawk would be honored each time lovers lay together by hanging a single black feather above the bed. Helina took to wearing a pair of the feathers in her long black hair as her crown. She would always be reminded of the part of herself that she liked, and it would temper her anger with a balance of wisdom and love.

Chapter 21

Fire

The decline of West was absolute. Disease of the flesh was the result of the terminally ill minds and souls of the people who had always lived in darkness. Evil lusters fought bodily weakness to live for sin and pleasure. Another day of existence for one purpose, ejaculation. There was no love for Baal, nor love at all in this darkest corner of earth. Fire was perpetual as fat and blood burned up the streets flooded with corpses. Charred bones protruded from black masses of burnt skin and hair. Flaming fluid streamed from the roof tops to the foundations. Smoky blasts of wind howled throughout and around the city like so many screaming ghosts of agonizing dead. Wails of pain and pleasure intertwined with the sounds of cracking red hot bricks. The blackened bloody fluid fell off to the sea in a boiling steam. Baal cracked and leaned but nobody noticed as the whole city caught fire in a conflagration of falling buildings and rising smoke. Those at the city's center were consumed with their new god as others were driven away by the heat. Blinded and burnt crowds ran for the sand hills and saw their city fall into a great fiery hole. There was nothing left. The survivors sat for days until thirst drove them in search of water. Fifty Thousand of one million were the people of West, and West was gone.

Fifty thousand homeless and hungry wretched people made their way west to the forest for there was no place else to go. They had hunting skills but feeding such a populace would be an insurmountable task and many thousands would die. They were thirsty and drank the blood of the fallen on the sand trails that snaked their way inland. The flesh of the sick would ensure that the strongest survived the exodus. The emaciated group consisted primarily of the street gangs who knew survival skills from a life of living on the fringes of society their entire lives. The gangs became even more cohesive and the people were divided by groups of boys or girls. The old were gone as were the very young. These wild packs of animal people walked together in an uneasy truce in search
of sustenance, but would fight amongst themselves from time to time along the way.

The forest provided them with shelter and animals where the camps of different gangs remained in close proximity to each other but with separate fires. The destruction of their city put a stop to the religious practices and their lust was replaced by hunger and thirst. They were still cannibals but the loss of the majority of their population caused the ancient instinct of survival to take over as they realized that they could soon eat themselves up entirely. Massive hunting of deer were organized and soon the groups started sharing. Virtually everyone took up the bow and arrow as they refocused their attention away from killing each other and instead sought out game to feed themselves. Thousands died from diseases acquired before the fire and the weak ones faded away. They began to fashion houses from the trees and for the first time became dwellers of the forest. Their hearts were not softened nor did they forsake the evil ways of the past, but that part of them was subdued for a time until they could rebuild their broken culture. After starvation, cannibalism and disease their number had dwindled to ten thousand young and strong males and females. They had no leader and were always suspicious of each other, but the truce persisted for the sake of life.

One of the toughest of the child gangs from the city had been a girl's group who were like wild dogs. They ranged in age from five years to twenty but the younger ones had succumbed to disease or starvation. They had a name for their gang unlike most for they stuck together, very unusual for any group from a culture whose ideologies centered around the self. These girls seemed to watch out for one another, not in a loving way but out of instinct, like a pack of wild dogs would hunt together. And just like a pack of dogs they had a leader who called herself Panther. She had long and straight flaming red hair with black eyes. Her skin was light and like all Westlanders, she had no body hair. She was tall and strong though lean from the lack of food. Panther was ruthless in a fight and would scratch the eyes out of her enemies sockets and shove her long black fingernails clean through the back and into the brain leaving the victim dying in agony. She was eighteen and had been on the streets all of her life. Young people joined with gangs for protection and survival and for all of them it was the only sense of family that existed. It was a family that could turn on you in an instant and destroy you but it was safer than the alternative of being at the mercy of adults in that wicked culture of West. Panther was feeling a sense of relief with the destruction of her city. She was limited in the amount of power she could attain as a gang leader among thousands of gangs. The territory was limited in the city and she liked the forest for she saw no end to the possibilities of attaining more power. For now she would focus her tribe on getting their strength back and developing the needed skills for survival in a much different environment. She was cunning and lustful, strong and beautiful, and her desires for power were unlimited. Panther was a great hunter unlike most of the children of West. She had stolen a bow from a soldier that she had killed for raping her. She had hunted in the dark alleys of the city, picking off her favorite targets, soldiers. She hated everyone and everything including herself. She had self inflicted scars on her neck and wrists. Her dress was a deer skin skirt and nothing else. Her bare breasts had markings of dried blood applied with her fingers each day and she rarely bathed. The bow was always on her shoulder and a deer skin pouch of arrows was slung from her waist. She never smiled but when she spoke, her teeth were sharp and white. She was as wild as any animal but her keen mind was her most deadly weapon. She loved fire and she was thrilled to see her city burn with all of the wretched people with it. Her gang was called "Death Bitches", and she was the undisputed leader. Their number was two hundred or so, and in this new environment of the forest they became the most feared group of all, and she was the most feared person of all.

The many gangs of the forest were getting settled into a

routine of hunting and building there own camps adjacent to one another. The males, who had dominated the Westland culture for millennia had placed their camps at the center of the new settlement with of course the females on the perimeter. It was still a male dominated society but now that the guards and the soldiers were gone their hold on power over the females was tenuous at best. For the first time in their history the men's dominance was in question but they were not even aware of it. The Death Bitches hated men as did the rest of the girl gangs. They hated Baal and were sickened at the site of soldier's naked wives at the phallus. It was the gang members who became the so called virgins of sacrifice and their hearts were full of revenge for the atrocities thrust upon them. Panther had a special hatred for all men and she sought to recruit more girls into the Bitches clan for strength. There were many unions of girl gangs being formed without the males being aware of it. The leaders of the opposing gangs would be taken deep into the woods and their throats would be slit. The members would join the bitches or suffer the same. Within a matter of weeks, there was one gang of females with one leader. Panther.

There had been a plan in the works for some time to destroy the boys and men of the Westland culture. Panther's love of fire inspired her to use it as a tool to burn them all. The men had been preoccupied with debating and fighting about who would be the new leader of all the gangs, and paid little attention to the activities of the girls. The Bitches would spend much of the day far away from camp presumably hunting. While they were hunting they were perfecting their archery skills and testing a new weapon dreamed up by panther. An arrow with a head of fire.

There were many horses in the woods that were used for ship building, and the girls practiced their riding and shooting day after day. They became very good at chasing and shooting deer in dense woods at a gallop. They did not use the fire arrows , not wanting to create smoke and stir the curiosity of the men.

One night most of the men were asleep and the girls crept quietly out of camp to gather a hundred waiting horses. A thousand Death Bitches formed a circle on foot around the camp with bows and arrows. A pile of flaming arrows was ignited and the horsewomen rode past it grabbing a single flaming arrow each. They ran a circle around the camp shooting the fire into dried brush that was laid out and surrounding the men. The circle of horses was continuously moving and a new flaming arrow was grabbed from the burning pile each time around and it in turn was delivered to an area that was not yet on fire. The men awoke within a complete circle of fire that was burning in towards the center. As they ran through the flames to escape, they were cut down with thousands of arrows shot from the girls on foot. The screaming men and boys followed by the sound of exploding corpses was heavenly to Panther. She had what she'd always wanted. She was the leader of the only gang and all of the bastard men had died a horrible death.

This new culture of women was without religion, or slaves, or ship building, or a desire to destroy Eastland. Panther could not care less about traveling across the sea to kill a bunch of cowards. Her domain was the forest and her army was ruthless. The female warriors were two thousand in number. They all had long straight hair that was either black, or red. They were tall and muscular and wore no breast covering, thus emulating their leader. They painted their fingernails black with tar and drew blood stripes across their breasts. Panther had a necklace of dog's teeth and a string of fangs around her waist. Her bravery and physical strength was admired by all of the girls and no one contested her leadership.

They left the charred camp of the men and headed ever deeper into the forest in search of wild horses. They became a traveling pack heading to the southwest, hunting deer and birds. After weeks of constantly moving, they came upon a small valley with a stream from which thousands of horses were drinking and resting. They set up camp and captured and broke enough of the horses so that every woman became an equestrian warrior. They had a common hatred for men and it was their nature to kill. Panther knew that her girls would need an enemy to conquer for they were of one mind when they were in battle. They left the small valley in search of war and traveled to the south hunting, and developing their skills as they went. Two thousand wild young women on horseback, long hair flying in the dust in the untraveled forest. Silent except for the pounding of eight thousand horse's hooves and heavy breathing. The dappled sun filtered through the canopy to the forest floor, appearing like a sea bed with the stream of creatures flowing by, winding through the brush at high speed. An eel aimlessly in search of a meal, or a snake slithering through the saw grass ran the line of horses and girls that looked as though it were a single entity. They were of one mind and moved thus, without a destination but anxious to arrive. Intent and purpose without a goal, all smiling at the thrill of it. Riding all day to stop only for water, until deep into the night by torch light. Hill after valley after hill after plain rode the deliverers of fire and death.

   Something unprecedented among any of the peoples from the evil culture of West began to happen. Perhaps it was the change in their environment, or the day after day of running on horses, or maybe the fact that the girls of the Death Bitches were of kindred spirits. It was like a single flower raising its face up in a field of bull nettle and thorns. This ruthless and cunning, heartless and violent collection of battle thirsty warriors were becoming a true collective. A bond was developing, indeed a sisterhood, a family in the truest sense of the word, arose from the ashes of the destruction of the wicked city, like a phoenix. They began to help one another and watch each others backs. At first it was a matter of survival that caused them to think of the group rather than the self. They found pleasure in one another's company and the strong would help the weaker. The older and wiser instructed the young and the sick were tended to like never before. They were not becoming weaker but stronger in this new found attitude of charity over greed. Each and every girl became precious and all followed the lead of Panther who encouraged this togetherness. The one, was important to the health of the many, and the many became one. They still had their deep hatred of men but there were no men around. The anger that had always kept their temperament on the verge of murder was gone, for the subject of their contempt was gone. The forest became beautiful as they rode each day. New color in the world revealed itself slowly until the trees and flowers exploded in a song that was new to their eyes. The sound of the wind and the blueness of the sky enchanted their spirits while the primordial feeling of oneness with nature invaded their hearts. Each day of their journey brought them closer to the land and each night brought them closer to each other. The pace of the horses began to slow as the weeks went by until the Death Bitches meandered along the forest floor with chatter and laughter in the dappled sunlight. They stopped to camp sooner each day, to build a fire, and their restlessness diminished in clearings under the canopy of the stars. They would comb one another's hair and they bathed more often. No longer were there blood stripes on breasts nor tar on nails. Smiles were abundant and amorousness was openly expressed with hugs and kisses. They had truly become sisters of the forest, lovers of each other and of nature. One day a girl of sixteen died from a fever, and the whole camp was in mourning. Her name was Rat, and she had become special as she was the youngest of the clan. They buried her by a brook under a willow. She was remembered in stories of her bravery and her skill at rock throwing. She was known for her habit of laughing loudly in battle which was assumed to be a tactic for subduing her fears. She was a little girl in many ways, but she was also a warrior of the Death Bitches. She would be remembered for a long time to come. The forest, a place full of savage beasts, yet these women had grown quiet, and introspective. They became aware of the need of the many, and of the individual. Panther began to think that the only reason that she was on the earth was for her sisters, and they all began to feel the same way, without it ever being said.

The wanderlust of the women began to diminish as their daily running of the horses became galloping and then walking. They traveled for fewer hours each day and would establish camp early and not break camp until deep into morning. They were among the largest trees that they had seen and they were captivated by the soaring height and amazing breadth of them. While resting beneath one, the girls decided to hold hands and wrap their bodies around forming a circle pressed tight against it. "Thirty three and one half girls!" exclaimed a warrior, and they all fell to the ground laughing and rolling in the deep leaves. The rest came running to join them in a riotous game of chase and laughter. They found healing in the woods with. The terrible past was vanishing and they found new life in this miraculous adventure. No one from West had known such joy and comfort from one another. No one had cared about the beauty of a tree or the humor in "thirty three and one half girls". These dregs of the dregs of the world, these murdering animals, had discovered a reason to live. Love, and laughter. The sun was beautiful as its rays shot down through the trees. A wind blew up and piles of golden leaves turned into swirling masses of color that rustled in the air. A boom of thunder was heard in the distance and the women made camp in this cavernous space formed by the giant trees.

No fires were built in camp as the knee deep dried leaves would have made it unsafe. Everyone made a bed out of the leaves, covering herself to keep out the night's breeze. The horses were sleeping all around the camp in a protective circle, and an owl hooted the girls to sleep along with the sound of distant rolling thunder.

The quiet night in the hollow made for a deep sleep full of dreams. Panther was at peace and walking by a bubbling brook with moss covered smooth stones on its edge. Yellow butterflies flew in dappled sun above the reflecting water. The heat of the sun was warm on her shoulders and hair as she daydreamed of a hot day in the city when she was a child. She was in an alley, tossing pebbles into a hole when a giant general approached her and asked where her mother was. She told him that she didn't know her mother. He grabbed her and threatened to eat her, and Panther started screaming in her sleep. She screamed in her mind so loud that she'd hoped that it would soon come from her mouth enough to awaken her from this lovely dream that had turned into a nightmare. She awoke on her knees screaming when she realized that the camp was engulfed in smoke. She yelled for everyone to get up and the horses bolted. There was total confusion as the women jumped from their beds to find themselves inside an inferno. Fire was moving through the camp so fast that some never knew it and perished beneath the leaves. Girls and horses ran in all directions, some into the fire that had surrounded the camp. Many climbed the huge trees to escape, as it was the only exit from the flames. They climbed many stories up to escape the fire and smoke, and several fell, succumbing to the heat. Panther saw that she was surrounded with no way out, when a flaming horse ran by and knocked her down. She grabbed the tail of the horse and held on as hard as she could. The horse dragged her at a full run through the flames that she thought would never end. Her skirt and hair were on fire as the horse kicked and ran in a panic. She never lost her grip and she hoped that the horse would not die before she could escape. She held her breath to save her lungs as she heard the horse coughing up blood. She closed her eyes and felt the intense heat baking on her fingers and face and she could smell the burning hair and flesh of the animal who never slowed down. They burst out of the flames and over the bank of a creek, the horse falling headlong into the water. Panther sought refuge on the far side of the creek as the flames flew overhead. She noticed that the smoldering horse was dead and floating in the creek. She could not hear the screams of people and animals for the roar of the fire, which forced her to lay underwater, coming up for a breath of hot smoky air when she had to. What seemed like a long time in the creek was only a moment, as the forest fire jumped the creek and continued its destructive path leaving only charred remains in its wake.

   Panther swam back to the shore and pulled herself up the black and muddy bank. The ground was still hot and smoking as she stood on her knees calling out to the girls. There was no answer but she heard moaning in the distance. She collapsed, with her legs still in the water and laid on her back to catch her breath. She could see the black smoldering limbs of the huge trees above her and her heart sank at the sight, knowing that many of her sisters had probably died. After she caught her breath she ran up the bank and into the blackened landscape in search of survivors. There was a great line of burned corpses with outstretched hands who had tried to outrun the flames but where unsuccessful. She wondered if she was the only survivor. A voice cried out to her from above and she saw three girls high up in a tree, clinging for their lives. The flames and smoke had not reached them and they were unharmed. They climbed down and the four searched for others. There were many corpses in the remains of burned out trees who were not so lucky and everyone that could be seen on the ground had perished under piles of leaves, many never having awakened by the fast moving flames. Soon other girls appeared from the direction of the creek, some badly injured but many with only singed hair and clothing. It appeared that most of the horses were gone as only a few dead ones were counted. Panther took a count of the survivors. There was sixty-two including herself. She led them all down to the creek where she instructed five girls to tend to the dozen or so injured. The rest went searching for horses and others who might have escaped the inferno. They found many more who had been on the edge of the catastrophe, having run in a different direction. Their number was now two hundred or more. They only found one more survivor after an hour of searching, and all were accounted for. She was badly burned from head to toe. Her clothing and hair were gone and the skin was melted on her face. She was found in the direction from whence the fire came and it was clear that she took a chance by running headlong into the flames, trying to reach the back edge of the conflagration, instead of out running it. There was no tree near for her to climb. The girls gathered around the pitiful victim and one of them held her hand. She was burned beyond recognition and no one could tell who it was. She gasped for air and writhed in pain as a single tear fell from her burned out eyes. Panther took up a big stone and crushed the poor girl's head mercifully killing her instantly, and for the first time, the Death Bitches wept.

Chapter 22

Dominion

   The Helenite's morning routine of giving thanks to the sun at the stone and wooden temple was never missed. The queen made it law that everyone attend the service. No excuse was tolerated, and the punishment would be stoning. She later made the exception for a girl in labor, not wanting to jeopardize the child's life. Her first priority was for the children to be fruitful when they came of age, and she would determine who the proper mate would be. She would have no courting rituals or love affairs, for she felt that those trivial luxuries were a hindrance, given the situation. Their numbers had dwindled substantially since leaving Eastland, and she stressed the importance of making new life. She instructed the hunters to be ever cautious, and take no chances. Even a minor injury could result in death, and if it meant losing a meal to be careful, it would not be the first time that they knew hunger. The group trusted their queen and obeyed her without question. She had a large house built for herself in a clearing half way between the pond and the temple, with smaller huts surrounding hers for the group. A fire pit was constructed in the middle with the boys living on one side and the girls on the other in a great square. They fashioned a wall of stones and spiked wooden posts that stuck out from camp. A trail went from the pond to the camp, and from there to the temple. She told the children that they lived between the water, which meant life for the body, and the temple, which nourished the spirit. They were not sure what the "spirit" was, as it was a new concept, and not even Helina knew, but she was depending on her intuition concerning religion and would trust the sun, the moon and the hawk to guide her.

Many of the children had come of age in a few months time, and she had done her best to pair them so that conception would occur without the love. Sometimes this strategy would be negated when a couple would grow attached to one another when she would have to split them apart in favor of other less likable partners. She found this plan to be time consuming and sometimes heart breaking. There had been no conceptions from the couples, and she became worried that the girls might be barren. She went to the sister moon to seek advice. She dared not consult the hawk, as he was a lover, and would offer traditional advice, and Helina was desperate. On the next full moon she made her way up to the temple alone to seek advice. She sat on the doorstep watching the moon on a crystal clear night. She emptied her mind and listened for hours without a word being given to her. Before morning she began to feel something that she had never felt before. It was like love but different. She closed her eyes and images of copulation flooded her mind and she could think of nothing else. A fire raced through her body and her genitals were full of sensation. She held her breasts and breathed heavy as the words came to her. "You must sacrifice your virginity for the sake of your people." The sister's voice was clear and sweet in her mind. "It is not the girls who are barren, but the seeds of the boys that come of age will need to be fertilized with my divine love through you. You must copulate with each one before they can create a new life with another." Helina was in shock at this revelation. She rushed back to her house without responding to the moon and thought about it for many days. She was very quiet for the next few weeks and some of the group asked her if she was ill. She shut herself up in her house and she began to realize that she would have to do as her sister had said. She grieved over the prospect of losing her virginity and at the same time became excited at the thought of a physical copulation. Soon she could think of nothing else but intercourse. Her eyes glazed over and her whole body tingled. She came out of her house and ordered that a fire be built for she had news from the sister moon. The group accepted what the moon had demanded and each boy would from this night forward, lay with the queen to become a man.

There was no longer any danger in the woods for the most vicious animals had been subdued. The dogs held their head down and ran each time that they saw a human and they would run off followed by a stream of arrows. The deer were thinning out from the hunters and other smaller animals made up a large portion of the groups diet.

There had been no rain in the months since their coming to the woods, and it seemed as though most of the moisture arrived in the form of dense fogs that crept over the land on most nights. It was a dry land but compared to the desert it was lush. One might the sound of thunder could be heard approaching from the west, and before morning a gentle rain fell, mixed with the fog. The misty weather went on for days and new plant life sprang from the ground. It was chilly and a fire was impossible to keep lit so Helina had a stone covered fire with a chimney built in place of the pit. They erected a covered area around the fire with a stone floor, which made for a cozy and warm place to eat and tell stories before bed. Everyone was in good cheer with the cool wet night around the fire, when Helina went to a boy named Narmu, who had just turned eighteen. She pulled him up by his hand and led him to her house and they closed the door behind them. Nobody seemed to notice even though he was still in her house when the daylight broke through the cloudy gray sky. The rain was falling a little harder and the landscape was turning to mud. As the day progressed, the rain increased to a steady downpour and streams of dirty water worked their way down the hill to the pond. The fire was quenched as wind blew water sideways into the covered fire place. All of the children remained in their huts for two days and nights to keep dry in the downpour. Helina and her lover were locked in an embrace of life giving passion until the rain subsided on the third night when a new moon was high. She took this as an omen that the moon had given her light to her, and she in turn had given life to the seed of Narmu. The young man went out and chose his mate that same day. His choice was Lili, a girl who was ready to come of age. His only attraction to her was physical. She was like a budding flower, ready to be pollinated, and she had the look of lust in her eyes. Their union would create twin girls, and Helina was convinced that the sister moon had given her divine advice. She perceived it as a union of the heaven and earth, through herself to create life. It was a glorious and lovely thing, and she worried no more about the groups dwindling population. Of all of the things that she had done for her children, of all of the sacrifices and guidance that had saved them from the many trials, this sacrifice of her body was the most difficult thing that she had done, but now ironically, it was becoming the most enjoyable to her, and she no longer missed her virginity.

It worried Helina that the deer population was thinning out

and she ordered a hunting party to make a scouting trip to the west to determine how far the woods extended in that direction and to see what the food situation was. She chose Narmu to be her new chief of the hunt and made him the head of her police as well. He was dedicated to her completely and at times she would have him sleep with her so that she would be sure that his seed remained strong. He chose eight of his best hunters to accompany him on the journey and appointed his most trusted friend Tep, to keep control of the camp in his absence. They set out before dawn and made their way through the wooded and hilly landscape that was green from the rains to determine the extent of their world. It was believed that the woods was another island in the desert for it was only a few days travel from north to south. Once before they had traveled under Lithair to the west for a day and a half but never found the edge of the woods in that direction. They knew that to the east, it was a short trek to the desert in that direction, and the only source of water so far had been the pond by their village. They were exploring the extent of their domain to determine just how long the woods could support their people which was sure to grow in population with the new system imposed by the sister moon.

Tep was a handsome lad, and Helina had watched him come of age with anticipation. It was time for him to be inserted with her life giving power and soon she would beckon him to her house. There were two others who had turned eighteen and she was puzzled over which one to lay with first. She thought to herself that as there would be more men to service, she would be busy indeed just performing the duties of channeling the moon's power. To save time she figured that she could copulate with more than one in a day, or perhaps several at the same time. It was logical, and it would leave her more time to govern. That evening she summoned the three young men to her house where they partook of her life giving body the whole night She saw this as her duty to her people but she found it so enjoyable that she would service many men simultaneously every night. To insure the fertility of each one would require regular visits to her house and she anticipated the other boys who would be coming of age soon. She would be their queen in every respect. They would obey her commands in and out of the bedroom and she liked this very much.

The girls of the Helenites where passive concerning the new procedures initiated by the queen, until a boy named Jason came of age. It was known by all that he and the girl, Suil, who was two years his junior, had been in love since they were little children. They were always together growing up and would be seen playing and talking together in the blue hills. They walked hand in hand on the silvery beach after slipping away from the campfires, where Jason would sometimes steal an innocent kiss. They would watch each others eyes and laugh about the overwhelming mutual crush that they felt. He would braid her hair and place flowers in it and she would wear his shirt all day to capture his smell. There love had been delayed by the many hardships in the past year, but now that life was beginning to get a sense of normalcy, their love became inflamed all the more. Helina knew of this and she had warned the couple against the union of lovers. They fought the urge to look at one another but could no longer resist. They were coming of age and their feelings began to grow ever more complex. They would never touch one another for fear of being seen and the police would always be vigilant about such transgressions. They would stare at each other during the morning ritual, instead of the tradition of staring at the sun with their eyes closed. It was against Helinas law to not do the staring during her chant when even she would have closed eyes. It was the only time that Jason and Suil could touch each other with their eyes, and they were taking a chance to do that.

One cloudy morning Helina came to Jason and took his hand to lead him to her house. Suil gasped an audible sigh, and The queen and Tep looked at her with surprise. Helina continued away with Jason, who did not look back while Tep showed a fist sized stone to Suil. It started to rain and Suil quietly sneaked from camp unnoticed to a hiding place where she cried all day. She sat beneath a willow that hung to the ground and hid her unhappiness. Her sorrow was such that she no longer wanted to live.

Jason beseeched the queen for many hours about retaining himself for Suil. Helina was ever so gentle with him while they debated the welfare of the people versus the desires of the one. She was not being seductive but rather, she was reasoning with him. Her argument was persuasive for she was armed with the words of the sister moon, but Jason's pure heart shattered her logic like a crystal goblet with one word. "Mik." Helina's face turned white and her shoulders slumped. She was speechless. "Remember your love for Mik? Remember when he and you were children, and you walked on the beach together, how you felt about him?" Jason's words were sweet and kind and he spoke with a nostalgia for love. " That was a crush that could have developed into something more, were it not for the events in our lives. His love for you was strong and he came for you. His quest cost him his life for there are some things in this life that one cannot live without. He has transcended into the hawk, and the wisdom of foolish lovers." Helina's feelings from that day, in the desert, standing above Mik's body, hit her like an ocean wave. She began to cry softly, realizing that the part of her that she liked best was still alive. " You truly are the voice of the hawk this night Jason. Go to your lover and be with her. Be happy together, and if the sister moon is kind tonight, you will conceive a child. If not, you will at least be happy.".

When Jason rushed from her house the rain had stopped. He looked all around the village for Suil, calling her name. He knew that there was only one place that she would be, and he ran for the weeping willow by the pond where she went to be alone. He slid down the muddy trail to find her but she was not under the tree. He saw her hair floating on the water and dove in to get her. He followed her blond hair to her face but she was not moving. He pulled her shoulders but something held her under. He discovered a bowstring around her neck and followed it to the bottom of the deepest part of the pond where it was attached to a stone. He chewed the leather into, and pulled her to shore and laid her on the bank. She had drowned herself out of grief. She was dead. Jason screamed the scream of a thousand hawks, and he laid with her body until morning beneath the weeping willow.

Jason would never forgive his queen for he blamed her for Suil's death. Helina tried to counsel him and she never again took him to her house, but his pain was such that he could never be happy again and he dedicated his life to helping young lovers in their cause. He became a mediator between them and the queen, which she respected. Whenever a case was made for the lovers, Helina and Jason would sit beneath the weeping willow and debate the moon and the hawk. His argument was always persuasive and he fought hard for the cause. Helina was open to the logic but she would eventually rely on her intuition to determine if it were the moon or the hawk who would speak to her heart. The queen admired Jason's keen mind and his passion for his cause, and deep inside, her feelings for him grew beyond admiration, but she knew that his feelings for her were limited to respect. They both learned much from their discussions as the doctrine of the new religion of the Helinites was being developed.

Narmu and his men had walked through the woods to the west for fifteen days without finding an end to the trees as they had expected. He began to wonder if their home was really an island after all. The landscape changed little with the gently rolling hills of brush with small trees of ebony and mesquite. They came upon several small ponds that were surrounded by willows that allowed them to replenish their water supply. Game was plentiful in the form of deer and hare, and they never saw a wild dog, which was a relief. Occasionally they came to a high hill where one of the boys would climb a tree to see what lie in the distance, but it was always more of the same landscape. One morning Narmu decided to change course and head north towards the desert and then loop back to the east on their return to the village. They arrived at the desert in three days and were astonished to see in the distance to the northwest, great mountains. The northern edge of the woods made a turn to the north and they could see the land rising up gradually from the desert floor.

The trees became larger on each successive hill to the horizon with the snow capped mountains towering a great distance beyond a magnificent forest. The hunters built a fire and camped for the night on the desert's edge. Narmu thought how like the ocean the desert was in the moonlight. The flat expanse glittered and seemed to move like flowing water. The sky on the north horizon turned like a wheel with a single star as its axis. He felt the earth moving beneath him and he wondered if it was not the earth that turned instead of the sky. Perhaps the sun did not come and go at will, but instead was still, in the sky. It made him question the idea of the sun as a being, rather than a thing, for it was he who was moving and not the sun. His mind wandered and wondered and he thought about the vastness of the night sky.

Was it like the desert with an end, or did it go on forever? Narmu thought about infinity, as looking at deep space can conjure these terrible questions with no answers. He wondered if he was committing blasphemy in doubting the sun's attributes so he thought no more about it. He laid on his back and enjoyed the colors of the stars as fell asleep.

The queen continued in her practice of sleeping with the young men of the village, but Jason had rekindled her thoughts about Mik. She would close her eyes and think of him during intercourse, and wondered if his spirit was in the bodies of her lovers. She lived this fantasy every time as she become convinced that the hawk was her lover. She found a contradiction between the hawk and the moon. Her mind began to reason that if she was possessed by the sister moon during sex, and her lovers were really the hawk, whose spirit was Mik's. Then who was sleeping with who? At times she felt betrayed by Mik, as he was really making love to the moon instead of her. Helina found this maddening. She was torn between her love for Mik, her lust for the young men, her duty to her people, her devotion to the sister moon, her anger at that sister for loving Mik, and her shame for her carnal feelings and loosing her virginity. Sex was very complicated for her indeed, and made for interesting conversation with Jason, under the weeping willow.

The sister moon's strategy was working. There were five new pregnancies in the village and more of the children were coming of age every week. Helina became very busy in her bedroom, and she decided that sleeping with the virgin men once should be sufficient to fertilize their seeds. Her new found fondness for sex was waning and she began to look upon it as a chore and a duty, and besides, she needed more time to consider other aspects of governing her people. One concern she had was Tep. In his zeal to police the village he and his boys had beaten some of the girls, and he was pressing charges against young lovers for flirtacious behavior with increasing regularity. Either her people were getting out of control, or Tep was getting out of control and she was unsure which was the case. She decided to spend less time in her bed and more time observing and even employed Jason as her spy to help her. Tep despised Jason though he hid his feelings well. Helina could see a potential for trouble and was hoping for Narmus' return soon. He was respected by all of the boys and men, including Tep, and she realized how important his presence was. An interesting form of government was developing for her new nation which filled her with both hope and anxiety.

Chapter 23

The Path

The Death Bitches were devastated by the forest fire. Their
number was a tenth of what it was, and they were reduced in
spirit as well. The camp was a scene of charred and twisted
remains of dead sisters and trees. This clan of tough street
thugs had found peace in the forest but that same forest had
turned on them in an instant, as soon as they had let down
their guard. They were filled with bitterness at the memory of
the dying girl that had to be killed mercifully. She represented
all of the suffering that these girls had endured, from the
alleys of West, to the cathedral of the forest campsite, and
their feelings of mistrust and hatred began to resurface. The
horror of the moment permeated their bodies and they fled
from the destruction in an organized frenzy of tears and
silence. Panther led the survivors out of the dark ashes and
into the green of the unburned forest. They found two
hundred horses that had escaped the inferno, and rode them
to the south for three days, only stopping for water. Weary
from travel, the ragged and smoke stained group made camp
in a large green clearing by a brook, far from any trees. They
foraged for roots and wild berries for dinner, bathed, and then
retired in the chilled night without the thought of a campfire
for warmth. It would be a long time before the word "fire" was
mentioned, and they began to wear more clothing at night.
They had washed the ritual bloodstains from their breasts in
the brook and refrained from that practice again. The smell of

smoke or blood became abhorrent to them and they only hunted when desperate for food.

After spending many months in the vast forest, they never saw a sign of other peoples until they happened upon a trail. Panther assumed that it was a path made by animals until she began to see signs of human activities. The first clue was an animal skin that had been fashioned into a water bag that was either discarded or dropped by accident. She filled the skin with water and it did not leak. The second sign was a thicket of brush that had been neatly cleared, and the path went right through it instead of making an easy detour. The girls rode softly and did not speak aloud for several days until the path became overgrown once more and had the appearance of an animal trail. It was a mystery that bothered Panther, and they doubled back to search the forest adjacent to the trail, to look for any other signs of humans. They saw nothing unusual until one of the girls noticed a small cave opening in a sheer rock wall behind some brush. It was just large enough to ride a horse through when she held her head down, and she noticed a dim light peaking through the darkness. She went back for the others and they all dismounted to investigate the discovery. The trail had been on an uphill incline for two days as it followed the bottom of a ravine with high cliffs on either side. When they had come out of the ravine that is where the trail turned wild again. One answer led to another question. Why did the trail end? The cave must be a passage to somewhere, but where, and for whom?

One of the girls, whose name was Kick, because she was a

good fighter with her feet, fashioned a torch out of dried grapevines. Her and Panther led the way into the cave on foot leading their horses. The others followed on horseback in a single file line. The cave remained narrow and the floor was smooth without obstructions. The torch illuminated crude drawings of animals on the walls of the cave in ochre and black, the entire length of the passage. Wind whistled through from the far side as the tunnel narrowed and then began to open up into a small cavern until they reached the exit that was much larger than the entrance. As they came out of the dark and into the light, they found themselves on a wide cliff overlooking an enormous valley that spread out to the west with a narrow river that snaked its way across the floor. Beyond the valley the land rose up to foothills at the base of a snow capped, mountain of granite. The air was cool and thin as they made their way down a path to the river where they rested on its bank for some time. The Bitches did not take well to the thin air, having spent their lives at sea level. Many found it difficult to breath and a few became ill as a sinking feeling of vulnerability permeated the camp. The river moved swiftly to the south that had to lead them to a lower land where the air was better, and after their rest, they mounted the horses and made their way along the bank.

The traveling was easy down the trail by the river and Panther drifted as the sun flickered on the rushing water with the bubbling sounds in her ears. The horses' pace was slow but steady and everyone was silent, enjoying the hypnotic effect of the dreamlike journey. Kick closed her eyes, as her horse seemed to know the way. There was a sweet smell of some pink flowers wafting along with the gentle cool breeze to their backs. Everyone was caught up in a euphoria so intense that time seemed to stand still. The sun was warm on their closed eyes and even the usual restlessness in the horses had subsided. They went on this way for hours until the sun began to set behind a hill and the cool air on their necks brought them back to reality. They had reached a bend in the river at a large flat clearing where the air was thicker and easy to breath.

Panther ordered a camp to be established where they would spend a few days. The water was deep at the bend and perfect for bathing, and there was shelter from the wind from a stand of poplars but there would be no danger of a fire for the wide-open field was on one side of the campsite while the river was on the other. They had learned a valuable lesson from the cathedral in the forest on where not to camp. A fire was built for the first time since the disaster with great care, making sure that there were no combustibles nearby. They were covered with dirt and stench from body odor and smoke. Panther was the first to slip into the cold deep and clear water of the bend in the river followed by the rest. It had not been the habit of this street gang to bathe yet the cleansing water was so inviting. The water was clear to the river's bottom, which could be seen even at dusk. It was made of smooth stones of every color and the girls dove down to retrieve some that were used to create a ring of stones around the campfire. Panther lay floating on her back and thought about all the things that had transpired since the destruction of West. She could not find the strength any longer to hate the men that they had killed and even felt remorse at the scale of the tragedy. Perhaps there may have been even one man that was worthy of sparing. Her thoughts turned to grief over the great loss of life of her sisters, the men, and even the city of West itself. Surely some of the people were not so evil, and besides, what made her less deserving of the same fate? Why was she alive now and floating on this lovely water on such a beautiful evening? She let out some of her breath and sank to sit on the bottom when a wave of guilt flowed through her that was like a waterfall within. She had never experienced this emotion with such intensity. Whenever any semblance of guilt had crept up in her, she had been quick to suppress it with the justification of revenge. Now that there was no longer anyone to hate, the focus of her feelings turned inward. Perhaps it was her all along that she hated and wanted to kill. Maybe she was as evil as anyone else in West, and should have died also. In the seconds when she was being pulled from the fast moving inferno by the burning horse, she'd had that very thought, to let go and to die, but her survival instinct made her hang on to that tail as if she were suspended above, from a great cliff by a rope. The event happened so quickly that her thoughts of death were an under thought that she was just now becoming aware of. "Why am I here?" she screamed in her head. "Why?" she yelled as the remaining air in her escaped with an explosion of bubbles. She opened her eyes from the bottom of the river to see the full moon in the sky, its image rippling with the surface of the water. She pushed hard with her legs to emerge like a dolphin, gasping for air. She swam to the bank and sat in the moonlight crying. All that she could think of was the poor burned girl's tears, and she felt her burning pain. She dug her fingers into the mud of the bank as she swore to herself that she would never kill again.

Panther wondered how it was, that she had developed such

a horror of blood and pain. As a child, she was abandoned into the alleys of the most despicable of places, full of violence and torture. A terrible feeling of abandonment had followed her all of her life that was like a fire burning her up from the inside out. She had masked the feeling with hatred, which manifested itself in the form of a reckless life. She'd followed her lusts to escape the pain of being deserted and she loved no one. She hated herself, mind and body, for that was all that she knew. Her scars of self-affliction were on her throat and heart, and the pain of loneliness saturated her being. There had been no hope in her life until this moment. She felt reborn out of the river, for as she had laid on its stony bottom, looking up to the moon, she saw clearly for the first time in her life, and it was painful and joyous at the same time. When she burst through the surface of the water, she left behind a part of herself that she hated in the stones below. She was a different person now, having survived the fire and now cleansed by the water. She walked to the campfire and lay down in the grass by the warmth of the ring of stones where she slept without dreaming for many hours. The morning awoke the girls with the sound of mockingbirds and the smell of lilacs. They were in the most lovely of landscape they'd ever seen and the sun was casting golden rays over the mountains to the east. Some of the girls fished in the river with bows and arrows and there was plenty to eat. Panther sat while munching her breakfast as she looked down the path by the river. The ground was golden from the sunlight, and yellow flowers with bees circling them were on either side. She felt a beckoning from this trail and she could hear it speak to her in the soft wind. Her people's destiny lies to the south, in the direction of the path. Everyone was refreshed and the horses were rested, she thought. It was time to follow that destiny, wherever it took them. She told the girls quietly to mount the horses for travel, and in short order they were on the move once more. Panther led the way followed by Kick, and as they rounded the bend in the river, the feeling that someone was watching them overwhelmed her. She was not afraid.

Chapter 24

The Stoning

The lovers of the Helinites, being unable to be with one another, began to take bold chances, as young lovers will. Tep, along with his police were always vigilant in search of transgressors of the law. An unauthorized affair had begun between one of Jason's assistants, whose name was Caron, and a young girl named Geenah. They tried in vain to resist the attraction between themselves and finally gave in by meeting late at night deep into the woods on a regular basis. They knew it would be a matter of time before they would be discovered and took great joy in each other's company. No one had ever actually been punished for breaking this law, for none of the couples had ever been caught. There were only three other couples that were taking such chances, but they did so only on rare occasions. Caron and Geenah's relation had intensified and they became more brazen, even in public where Tep had seen them holding hands while they ate their dinner. He decided to focus his attention on them and he stayed up all night to investigate whether or not the young couple was indeed having sex.

Tep did not tell the queen about his plan, and he hid outside the village in a high and hidden spot where he could see all comings and goings. He did not have to wait long, after everyone retired, he saw Geenah slip out of the back of her hut, and crawled away into the darkness. Soon after, Caron followed. Tep ran to get three of his helpers and the four went into the woods in pursuit. They followed the couple as if they were stalking a deer, without making a sound. He was surprised at how close to the village that the couple decided to have their meeting, as it was only two hills beyond it. The police sat quietly in some brush and watched the lovers in their passion. They waited until the two were completely engrossed in each other when they ran out and grabbed them at the moment when they would least be watching out for trouble.

They were bound, blindfolded and then tied to large sticks to be carried back to the village like captured prey. The returning ruckus awoke the entire village and Helina came out of her house to see what was happening. She was greatly disturbed not only about the discovery of the crime of the lovers, but also at fact that they would have to be punished for it. She knew that these poor children would suffer terribly, and she also knew that the law must be executed and the sooner the better. The rest of the village became angry at the prospect that their brother and sister would soon die, and they beseeched Helina for mercy, but her ears were closed. She had a problem on her hands and she wished that Narmu were present to help out with the strength of the other hunters who were with him.

Jason immediately intervened on behalf of the accused and a debate began in the village center about what would happen next. The crowd was behind Jason as he talked of the hawk and spoke for all lovers. Helina removed herself from the debate and retreated to her house not wanting to be influenced by Jason's persuasion. Tep spoke the law on the queen's behalf, stating that it meant the very survival of the Helinites. The law was given to the queen by the sun and moon. The law was inflexible and the law must be upheld without delay. "The children shall be stoned to death by the collective. They will be tied to a stake in the middle of the square and each and every man; woman, boy, and girl will throw a stone with force to kill. If any does not throw their stone with force, they too will be stoned." Tep was stern in his oration and many of the girls began to cry. The lovers were tied to a stake back to back with their blindfolds still on. The queen watched from her window and cried in the darkness when she realized that Tep was right. The crowd gathered in a large circle around the condemned, and each took up a stone to throw. Tep knew that the people would be reluctant to kill so he told them that by not striking the lovers with a hard blow, would only prolong their misery, even though the punishment was meant to be brutal and painful. The first boy threw his rock, hitting Caron in the foot. He made no sound but Geenah began to sob uncontrollably yelling that she was sorry and would never break the law again. Tep replied that the law was broken and that she must pay with her life. She became hysterical as the second stone struck her knee lightly and bounced off. "Throw your stones!" yelled Tep, and a few more hit the boy in the chest. This process was turning out to be slower than Helina could bear, but she remained silent in her window. Only one or two stones were thrown every time Tep screamed and he was beginning to enjoy the power of the moment. He felt as though he was the one and only stone thrower for it was his thoughts and voice that made the pain come ever so slowly. He noticed one young girl who had no stone to throw and he took one and placed it in her hand. She looked at it and then at Caron and Geenah, and she dropped it to the ground without a word or gesture. Tep grabbed her by the hair, dragged her through the dirt and tied her to another stake in the ground not blindfolded. He stood back and picked up a large stone and crushed her head three times until she was dead. Helina turned away.

The group became fearful and started to throw the stones, slowly at first and then faster. They aimed for the legs, which broke quickly. They then started throwing toward their heads. But their aim was not true. Suddenly a man ran out of the dark and held up his hands for everyone to stop. The children cried out Narmu's name as he untied the couple and laid them on the ground. "Water!" he yelled. Everyone dropped their stones and a few ran to get water for the condemned lovers, and when Narmu checked the fallen girl he noticed that it was too late for her. Her skull was crushed. Helina came out of her house and watched without saying anything as Tep admonished Narmu for his transgression. "I do not care what the law says. When I am around, no child shall die or suffer. That is my law. You Tep shall die by my hand for killing this girl." Narmu's voice was like thunder as he walked toward Tep. He pulled the stake from the ground that had held the dead girl and shoved it through Tep's chest and into the ground. The children circled around him and pelted his dying body with stones until he was buried under a pyramid with the shaft of wood sticking out of the top. Helina smiled at this turn of events as the children tended to the lover's wounds and kissed their faces. Tep's police force faded into the back of the crowd and said nothing as Narmu's men watched them with great interest.

Helina spoke to the children; "Narmu is my right hand and a servant of our religion and laws. He saw that Tep was wrong and a criminal, and he did what was right. The sun has shown mercy on the lovers this day, but I caution you to not break the law for lovers until the moon speaks to me once more. We must not tempt the gods for they will kill as readily as they show mercy, as you have witnessed today. That is my judgment." Jason and Narmu embraced one another and then Helina. "Thank you Narmu, and you my queen" Jason whispered to them.

Everyone went back to their huts for the night and Helina brought Narmu into her house to discuss his journey and to enjoy his company. It had thrilled her to see her muscular hunter kill Tep. She had developed a hatred for him, and was happy that he was no longer alive, but more than that, she became excited at the site of his violent and bloody death. She lavished kisses on Narmu's face and chest and then licked Tep's splattered blood from his hands. Narmu did not resist but found her behavior disturbing and ghoulish. She pulled him to her bed where they made love all night as she moaned with delight while scratching his back with her fingernails. It was the most satisfying sex that she'd had and her appetite was insatiable. The morning broke with the lovers embraced in sleep where they remained for the rest of the day.

Chapter 25

Weapons

Narmu and Helina awoke to the sound of children laughing, and they remembered the night before. "How lovely their voices are, so full of happiness and hope" Helina said softly. "The right thing was done. I feel it deep in my bones that it is wrong to harm them no matter what they do. Tep had to die, for he descended on a dark path by his choosing, one of murder and hatred" Narmu replied. Helina hoped so, but her uncertainty grew for trying to guess what the gods desired was a dangerous game. She had seen the power of the sun when he destroyed the soldiers from West, and she remembered the controversy that existed between the hawk and sister moon. For now though she was happy in the arms of Narmu, the first love she had known since her unrequited love for a dead man. She kissed the bleeding scratches on Narmu's back and recounted the beauty of his magnificent murder of Tep. She could not purge from her mind the image of his surprised and helpless face after the stake had been driven through his chest. The blood was redder than she'd seen before, and the children's pummeling him with the stones was more than she could have hoped for. She kept these thoughts to herself, and just told Narmu what a brave man that he was. She was slowly developing a mania for the morbid that she could share with no one. It was the part of her self that she hated, but the darker her thoughts became, the more she became engrossed with the horrible.

Helina was pulled away from her reverie when Narmu began to recount his journey to the west. He told her about the desert's edge that curved to the north, and there he saw great forests and mountains to the west. He described the promise of an abundance that they had not seen since leaving Eastland. "A great spirit called me from an endless space, to bring our children out of these woods and into a new life of happiness and peace. I watched the earth spin like a ball and felt touched by a mere second of eternity. It is our destiny Helina, and we must follow it". Narmu's soft words entranced Helina with visions of a new land where her people could grow into a great nation. She pictured herself on a throne, surrounded by her obedient subjects with Narmu to her right, and Jacob to her left. It all seemed to make sense now, from the attack of the soldiers to their trek through the desert and into the woods. They had changed much in such a short time, but it was their destiny. The sun, moon and hawk were guiding them on this ascent to enlightenment as Helina's mind made its descent into an abyss of darkness.

"We shall leave in the morning!" Helina proclaimed. Narmu rushed from her bed and into the square to make the announcement and then began shouting kind, but firm orders to break camp.

There was excitement in the air as the children made ready for the next part of their voyage. They were still a nomadic group so little that needed to be done beyond the packing of clothing. The hunters would provide food as they went and there were plenty of small ponds to drink from on the route through the woods. Special wooden beds were constructed for carrying Caron and Geenah, and four girls were assigned to their care but all would share their burden. Traveling always brought the group closer together and they became a true collective during times of stress.

It was two weeks of easy travel before they arrived at the desert's edge, but the mountains to the west could not be seen because of clouds in the distance. They camped that night in the sand for a change from the woods, and many of the younger children played games and ran about laughing. Helina called for a fire to be built at sunset and decided to have a storytelling. This had not been done for a long time, and the children were eager to hear what their queen would have to say.

The night was especially dark with cloud cover as the group had formed a near perfect circle around a large fire was mostly embers and small yellow and blue flames. The desert wind was refreshing and the smell of the smoke from ebony wood was intoxicating. Helina stood uncharacteristically for the telling as she usually sat on the ground to be on the level of the listeners, which had been the tradition of the elders. She walked over to the fire as close as she could get without discomfort and stared into the flames for quite some time. Everyone was silent and the only sounds were that of the light wind and the cracking of the burning wood. Her black hair shone blue in the firelight and her eyes were the color of the ebony wood. Yellow flames reflected from her black eyes and translucent skin and at times the fire seemed to emit from within her. She began her talk very slowly and quietly, but loud enough to be heard by all.

"We embarked on this journey of ours almost two years ago. Our world has been both cruel and giving. You have grown much in your quest for survival and have had to sacrifice love, for life at times. Now we have come full circle and once again, we have both love and life. We are stronger than we have ever been and we have sacrificed much to gain wisdom. This fire of ebony is like us. It consumes itself to survive, and when the wood runs out, the fire dies. You are all like individual fires in this life. When your ebony is gone, so you will be. If your fire dies though, fire itself remains in the world. They all have a beginning and an end, but a new fire will always be born. We are a part of each other in this way. Sometimes the fire grows out of control and can cause great harm. That is when it must be extinguished, as Tep was extinguished. His fire was out of control and threatened to wreak havoc. It is important to remain a part of the collective and not to spread your flame beyond yourself, or you also will be extinguished. You must trust your queen from now on and do as my laws command, for I alone speak with the gods and understand how we must live and think. " Her voice grew louder, " Together our flames combine to be a conflagration that is powerful. We must burn together as one, and not as individual flames, for alone, your fire will burn out quickly, but together we burn for eternity. We go to a new place in the morning and we know not what dangers await us. It is a land of abundance and hope, but where there is abundance, there is always peril. When there is hope, there are always risks. Let us be as one, and together we will conquer our fears and enemies. Be not afraid to kill if you are asked to, for to kill, sometimes means to preserve life. Be not afraid to die if you are asked to, for to die, sometimes means to preserve life as well. Sleep well tonight my beloved children, for tomorrow we burn as one, on our way to becoming a new and powerful nation. We are the Helinites!" Helina's voice was loud and clear when she ended her speech and it echoed into the desert, as the flames appeared to fly from her outstretched hands. The children became convinced that their queen was truly a goddess, and the master of their lives.

Before retiring, Narmu asked the queen for an extra day before setting out toward the mountains. "We will need to replenish the arsenal with more bows and arrows, and we should prepare the group for self defense if needed. She granted his request and held his hand in the dark where no one could see. "We must not show our affection in the open Narmu. We don't want to give the children any ideas of their own." Narmu agreed with her and they slept on opposite sides of the camp.

With morning came intensive training and target practice for the warriors and hunters, while the youngest children sought out the perfect wood to be used for their weapons. Everyone was proficient at archery but most had not used it since the war with the dogs. One more night of rest and they were off before sunrise, following the edge of the desert as it curved to the northwest. When the sun began to rise, the group stopped dead in their tracks at the clear and spectacular view of the mountains on the horizon. They seemed so close but it was a full, four days travel to the foothills and the piney forest. There was excitement in the air and their steps were lively with the anticipation of a promised land finally coming to fruition before their eyes. They began to think as one like never before, and they even walked in unison like soldiers going to war. They had all forgotten about making love and playing games, replacing those seemingly trivial pursuits with patriotism and honor. Every last one would now do as Helina said, even unto death. They were the Helinites, the greatest army in the world and the masters of all living things. Nothing would stop their resolve now and victory would be theirs. But victory over what, some wondered to themselves?

Travel was easy for the group skirted the edge of the woods the entire trek so that they could easily find water and game. Hunting allowed for more practice with the bow, and Narmu allowed the younger ones to venture out to hunt as they walked along without loosing sight of the group. For the first time there was a sense of adventure instead of mere survival, and everyone was content. The closer they came to the mountains the more they could smell the smells of the forest. The piney aroma blew in from the west along with the sweet smell of fresh, cool water. They could see rain clouds beyond the foothills and a beautiful rainbow appeared. It was like a great colored gate, inviting them into a paradise, lush and green. As they approached the western edge of the desert, where the green grass began, the purple granite color of the mountains became vivid and glowed with the reflecting sun. Snow-capped peaks jutted upwards into the clouds, and it looked like a home for gods.

They made camp in a green meadow at the base of the foothills near a cluster of pines. Although the children of East were lovers of the sea, they also missed the mountains and blue rolling hills that was just as much a part of their daily lives. The desert had been a new and challenging experience for them, but they felt comfortable in this new place. Narmu gave orders for no one to stray far from camp for they did not know what new dangers this land might have. Everyone was tired from the traveling and went to sleep just after sunset without even building a fire. A screaming child in the distance awoke Narmu in the middle of the night and he jumped up with his weapon almost instinctively. He yelled for his troops and off into the dark night they ran. The child's voice came from the forest and it became more a voice of agony than a cry for help. They reached a small clearing to see the horror of a black bear thrashing the dying child about in its jaws. The men fired arrow after arrow at the bear and most of them splintered on impact and bounced off. The bear dropped the child and charged the men as they kept firing their arrows, aiming for the eyes and mouth. Thirty arrows hit the bear without slowing it down until one of Narmu's hit it square in the left eye, dropping it in its tracks. They rushed to the poor boy of ten years to aid him but it was too late. The bear had ripped his little body and crushed his skull. "His fire has burned out," Narmu said as he gathered his bloody corpse to his chest. The men rushed back to camp with one thought, to protect the rest of the children.

Everyone in camp cried for the little one whose name was Jem. Helina ordered that his body should be burned to keep the bear from returning for it, so a ceremony of death was held in which all who had something to say about poor Jem could do so. It was a somber occasion of reality. This paradise had monsters hiding in the darkness, lying in wait to eat the unsuspecting. "This," Narmu said with tears in his mouth, "will never happen again. I swear it."

After the burning of Jem, camp was moved back to the desert where guards were placed around the perimeter. At least they could see what danger was approaching in the open spaces. The dogs in the woods was a terrible tragedy, and a glorious victory for the Helinites but the bear was a nightmare from hell, a demon devouring young children. It was a monster the color of the night that was silent until it had you. The sleep was restless for all, and many laid awake shivering with fear or crying for poor little Jem.

Narmu stood guard and contemplated the problem of his arrow's inability to stop the large beast. There had been small bears in Eastland, but they had never attacked a human, as all the animals were passive. This land was savage and humans were just as much food as hares were. He knew that if they were to go forward into the mountains, they would need a better weapon than the flimsy arrows. They worked fine on the dogs, but the bear's skin was like stone, he thought. Throwing rocks at this bear didn't seem to Narmu like a practical solution. There must be an answer. We cannot return to the woods and live like the dogs forever, eating hare and snakes. This land is promising and we cannot give up before we even enter into it, discouraged by the first beast that we confront, as formidable as it is. We are the masters of our domain, which is wherever we go. His thoughts raced through his mind while he kept a keen eye on the edge of the forest. "I must find a way". He envisioned the sharp stones that they had used to skin the animals they had killed. He thought of the uselessness of their arrows. It was one of those moments of discovery when the solution to a problem seemed elusive, that very second when the brain becomes aware of the answer, "Attach the sharp stone to a large stick for thrusting", he said to himself.

Panther and Kick were telling silly stories to pass the time while they led the girls down the trail by the river. The path led them downhill, following the river's flow, through meadows and fields. They came to a thicket of thorns that had grown over the trail so dense that they had to beat it aside with large sticks in order to get through. This went on for some time and other girls took the lead to relieve Panther and Kick. The sound of the river became louder as they made their way through the dense growth until it was a roaring noise that had to be a waterfall. When they finally broke through, the scene was a spectacular vista of a huge valley that stretched on to the horizon. The water fell a great distance from the precipice on which they stood to the basin below. It was a fantastic panorama of color and light with the river winding through green fields surrounded by a lush and tropical forest. A rainbow was ever present from the mist that was created by the falling water bouncing off of the craggy cliff on its way down to a clear and green pool. The sky was bluer than any that they had seen before, with small white clouds that created a pattern into the distance.

Panther heard a hissing noise from nowhere and Kick fell at her feet dead. She saw the arrow sticking from her chest and immediately pulled it out. It had a tip of stone that had penetrated her breast and entered her heart. Everyone retreated to the thicket and readied their bows as Panther looked at the weapon, the likes of which she had never seen. "A stone" she said aloud. She clutched it in her fist and ran for cover.

The girls hid in the brush, staring out into the lovely landscape with the dead body of Kick, bleeding and all alone. There was nothing that could be done for her now. They lay hidden for the longest time and the only sound was the water spraying off of the rocky cliff in its descent to the pool below.

The attack had been one lone arrow. Panther decided that it was too dangerous to move out of the thicket and down into the valley below. There was an enemy waiting that could not be seen. It could be a thousand warriors or a lone boy, and the single, silent attack left her in agony about what to do next. She decided to not take any chances and ordered a retreat back up the trail to the meadow where they had camped. Here they would devise a plan, she thought, and also make some arrows with tips of stone instead of their traditional ones with a sharpened shaft of wood with tar soaked twine just below the tip to give it weight and balance. The women from West went into battle mode once again after having drifted away from their hardened ways for a time. They had learned much about the human heart and had grown a new compassion for one another. They even felt remorse for their atrocities and had begun to see a new world of light and color within themselves. The sisterhood that developed was making them think as one, with Panther, the one whose spirit and mind seemed to have evolved by generations in the short span of months as their leader. They did not build a fire but sat in the starlight in a large circle facing outward and touching shoulders. They did not sleep or speak the whole night, and the sky turned above them as they meditated in a collective conscious without thought. They were determined to survive, but not with the bloodlust and anger of vengeance that they once possessed. The concept of calculation and patient endurance had now replaced murder and lust. They no longer wished suffering on anyone after witnessing the unknown burnt girl's death. They had felt her pain and despair as she chocked on her last breath of life. They knew that they lived in a haunted land with a life of demons and darkness and they no longer wanted to contribute to the hopeless world but rather, bring light to where there was the dark and to bring hope to where there was none. They had become one with that wretched girl as they held her hand and saw her tear fall. They felt compassion and empathy with her and now they could visualize the consequences of their actions. They would try to avoid the terrible and the evil that they had always been. Even now with the potential for a war with an unknown enemy, they would consider the cost of it, not only to themselves, but to the attackers as well. A life was taken from them in an instant and they were angry and missed her, but to kill for revenge would be a second injustice. There must be a way to avoid more death and sorrow, Panther thought, and they all thought the same thing at that same moment while the love of life and the love of themselves was beginning to dominate the collective mind of what once was the Death Bitches.

The group sat in the circle all of the night, saying nothing. They watched the stars and listened to the bubbling water of the river. At sunrise they ate a breakfast of berries and water. Panther began speaking to the girls as they ate. "We are all of one mind now as I felt your feelings during the night. We must survive this haunted world that we were born into. We have survived in the past by the pain of others. That is the way of this life. If you observe the animals that devour each other to live, they do not kill each other for revenge or for pleasure as our people always have. Our home had slipped into a chaotic and self-absorbed culture of something unlike the world of the animals. Ours was truly a life out of balance, and that is why it fell into a fiery hole. As dark as the world is, it would not tolerate the dread of our people. We have come far from that night of obliteration and penalty so let us now, not slide back into that abyss. Let us not retreat though, back to the forest of fire. There is promise in this land we have discovered and we are in desperate need of men to continue ourselves." The word "men", startled the group and some let out an audible gasp. The memory of rape and torture were scars on the souls of every one in the tribe and some even cried at the thought of even facing another man. Finally the sister, whose name was Shasta, stood up to speak her mind. " We are of one mind for all that you say Panther, except for that. That word you spoke makes my head hurt and my vision dim. It hits my heart like the arrow that struck Kick. Say it again and surely the blood will leave my body like Kick as well. I know that I speak for many here if not for all on this matter. We abhor them and their stench of feces and urine. They made us into animals, and now that they are dead we live with hope and dignity and a love for one another". Many of the girls stood in unison with quiet support of what Shasta had said.

"I too have a dark spot in my heart from the abusiveness of soldiers since I could remember. I have dismissed the thought of them my entire life for it sent me into a rage that I could not control. I am different now as we all are. If we, the darkest of girls could transform as we have, into loving creatures, then surely there must be men in this world that are of a gentler nature than the men from our culture. Surely there is someone who is like us who will mate with us", "How can you speak of mating?" Shasta said with her voice raised. The thought of such a sickening image made several of the girls vomit and many cried from thinking about past abuses.

"We were brutalized, each and every one." "My sweet Shasta. We ourselves were equally brutal lest you forget. We are they! We murdered them! We are no better. No more talk of that now for there is something more important that we face this morning. Do we go into the valley to seek revenge for poor Kick as we sought revenge on the raping men of our own people, or do we find another way to try to avoid more bloodshed?" "How can bloodshed be avoided!" exclaimed Shasta. "We have been victims of a brutal society our whole lives. That has ended because we had the strength to destroy those who treated us as animals. The filthy beasts, the men of our culture had to die that we might live. Are we to now let those live who have killed our beloved sister? I say we destroy them all"! The group was beginning to divide on the issue at hand and Panther knew that she had to calm them before things got worse. "Have we learned nothing? Are we to digress to the sorry state from whence we came? Who among you would return to the slaughter? Who among you would prefer to live a life of perpetual murder? I say there is more to this world than mere survival. Look around you at the beauty of this land. I say that the world is not haunted of itself, but by the killers that dwell in it. If we become the Bitches once more, we become the haunters, no better than the poor wretched souls that lie at the bottom of the fiery hole that was West." "How then sister, do we proceed? Do we turn around and go back to the forest to live in fear of the fire, or do we conquer this valley for our own and kill the ones who murdered one of us? Shasta's tone was quieter and the group listened intently for the response. "I say that we adopt a double strategy. One of peace but backed by one of self-defense. We are the invaders to this place and perhaps the people who live here will listen to reason and allow us to lay claim to part of this valley. Let us make arrows with tips of stone, but let us also make a plan to seek out the aggressors to try and come to a compromise. They may be a peace loving people who fear us. We know nothing of them. I will go into their realm in search of an answer. Who will go with me?" "I will", said a soft and little voice from the back of the group. "I will go with you Panther to seek peace". Everyone was astonished to see that it was Peek, Kick's blood sister who was only twelve years old.

The one person in the clan who should have wanted revenge was the first to join Panther in her quest for forgiveness. Little Peek, who was no less abused and abandoned than the rest, was the one tiny voice to speak up in a fight against bloodshed. Her long blonde hair was stringy and a smile peeked through a face dirty with berry juice. A tear rolled down her cheek and caught in the corner of her mouth as the group circled around her. "I do not want to be a haunter", she said softly. The girls rushed towards her, their hearts aglow and embraced her with gentle kisses. "We do not want to be haunters either", said a voice from the crowd.

Chapter 26

Narmu's Revenge

The resolve of the Helinites grew as everyone's thoughts were on the terrible death of Jem, especially in Narmu who had made up his mind to kill the culpable bear. He went into the forest alone in search of a stick that he could use to fashion the weapon of his revenge. He cared not for his own safety and his focus was on the object of his search, never glancing over his shoulder for danger. Most of the trees were not suited for the purpose for he needed a stick of great hardness. He searched the whole day, venturing deeper into the piney woods, not noticing the beauty of the place or the bounty of its wildlife and vegetation. There were hare; deer, squirrel and birds everywhere, but he never even saw them. His mind was fixated on the task at hand and he even tried to put Jem out of his thoughts so that he could focus. Many pieces of wood were discarded after they easily broke across his knee until he came upon a clearing, a green meadow with a lone tree, the likes of which he had never seen. "You, black and burnt tree that yet lives", he said aloud as if the tree were a person. "Why do you stand alone for me in the midst of this meadow? What spirit is in you that you would plant yourself here for me many years ago, knowing that one day I would come for you"? Narmu yelled at this tree that had suffered many fires in its life but still had a full crown of green. He pulled on a branch and found that he could not break it. The twisted limbs were not suitable for the most part but for one that was a third of the way up the short trunk. It was as straight as an arrow and had the length of the height of a man. "You shall be the instrument of my revenge, and together we will kill the night beast that is the horror of our lives"! Narmu continued yelling as he climbed. "Your black skin covers a heart of stone that I must have. I only want a part of you to replace the part of me that was taken. I will use you for a good purpose, to kill the killer of one of my children. You tell me that I am right to kill this beast or you would not be here. The father sun has given you life for years, to make you grow for this purpose. I will kill for Jem and my people. I will kill for my god the sun, and I will kill for myself because it is my pleasure". Narmu was jumping up and down on the straight branch with all of his might and weight. "I will kill this beast and all others like him", he screamed as the limb gave way with a crack that echoed through the forest so loudly that all in camp heard it. They knew in an instant what it was and everyone smiled with the thought of revenge in their hearts. "The black beast will die", said Helina. The branch splintered as it broke under the pressure of Narmu's pounce and he fell to the ground in a tumble. He struggled as he fell, to land on his feet but another limb struck his head that knocked him out cold before he hit the ground. When he came to, the hot breath of the black bear was on his face. He leapt to his feet with the broken branch in his fists and began to hit the beast in the mouth until it retreated. The bear circled around Narmu with its teeth exposed in a sneer as he flipped the stick around with the freshly broken sharp end pointing in its direction. The bear charged on all fours again and again as Narmu thrust the spear into its mouth and eyes with each attack. The bear stopped for a moment, glared at the man, then stood upright and ran at him with all of its weight and speed, mouth wide open. Narmu charged in its direction with his lance gripped firmly and shoved in down the bear's throat with all of his strength. The bear convulsed in agony on the ground for several moments, trying to pull the stick out of its bleeding mouth with its paws. It cried in pain and stood up to attack but fell immediately to its side in misery. The man took up a large stone and crashed it down on the animal's head repeatedly, calling out Jem's name with each strike. The bear was bleeding and spinning around on the ground in agony as it tried to crawl away from its inevitable defeat. Sweat poured from the man's body while blood from the beast splattered in every direction. It took a long time for the large animal to die and Narmu was amazed at how much effort it took from him to take the life from this now helpless monster. He could hardly lift the stone from exhaustion as the last few blows silenced the enemy for good. Narmu fell to his knees and began to cry for little Jem and he spit upon the bear. He felt a sharp pain in his stomach and fell on his back as if he were knocked down. His agony intensified as he slowly reached for the pain in his stomach when he felt the warm fluid of his own blood running down his side. His fingertips followed the blood toward his navel when he felt the hardwood weapon he had used, sticking out of his belly and pointing to the sky. "How did this happen," he thought. I do not recall being injured, in fact, I killed the bear with this very stick". Narmu could not move a muscle besides his right hand and fingers. He listened for the bear or any other sound when he heard the lovely singing of a mockingbird. He could only see straight up through the trees where a lone white cloud drifted slowly by as a placid breeze made the leaves of the hardwood tree dance gently. His pain was terrible and he realized that he was impaled by the very weapon that he'd used to kill the beast. He thought out the last moments of his life trying to make sense of what had happened. He had no memory of his injury and it seemed as though time itself was missing from his life. He used all of the senses trying to make sense of this enigma. He could not smell the dead bear but only the smell of his own blood mixed with the scent of lilacs. He could not move and he realized that he was dying as his blood emptied from his body. His vision grew dim and the pain in his stomach subsided, then all went black.

Helina became worried as the sky grew dark and she decided to search for Narmu in spite of the mortal danger of the darkened forest. She chose three hunters to accompany her without preparation and headed into the blackness of the woods leaving the starlit desert behind. The sound of the cracking wood began to worry her as the group hastily made their way towards the direction that the sound originated. Her mind was not on the bear or Jem, but focused on Narmu. She thought of the hawk and called out to him for help in finding her lover. She beseeched the sister moon for her kindness and to the father sun for strength. They began to run at her urging as she thought about Mik, and how he'd died while searching for her. She could not bare the thought of another dead lover and she knew somehow, that Narmu lay dying.

As they came to the clearing of the green meadow she saw his body lying beneath the hardwood tree with the stake sticking up from his gut. She fell on him crying and tried to stop the bleeding with her hands around the wound but no blood was flowing. His body was cool and he had no breath. His eyes and mouth were wide open and she kissed his parted lips when she realized that he was a corpse. Her anger was explosive as she placed her foot on his belly and yanked the weapon from his wound, then held it over her head and screamed that she would avenge Narmu.

Helina was a madwoman with glazed eyes and gritting teeth. She was an animal on the prowl of the killer beast, and nothing would stop her. Sharp stick in hand and arched back, she circled the area in search of the black bear in the dark night. The hunters were frightened of her and followed cautiously behind. She lunged at every shadow and every bush. She stopped from time to time to listened, and then ran like a maniac from tree to tree in search of the killer, driven by a murderous revenge that she had never felt. She grunted and howled and sniffed the ground like a starving animal with her long red hair flailing. This went on all through the dark night until at last her lunge into nowhere struck the fur of the invisible monster. It came toward her in a run on its hind legs with white teeth glistening and hot breath on her face. She ran with all of her might with the weapon in her fists as her feet left the ground. She buried the stake into the beast's skull with such force that it came out the back carrying brains and bone with it. It was dead before it hit the ground.

Narmu awoke on the ground beneath the hardwood tree with the sun in his eyes as a dragonfly lit on his nose. He felt for the wound in his belly but it was not there. His head hurt and he rose up dizzily when he'd realized that he had been knocked out from the fall from the tree, and that his fight with the bear was a dream, indeed, Helina's fight with the bear was a dream as well. His wound was a dream. He jumped up from the ground to confront the bear and then started to laugh, as there was nothing around him but the tranquil green meadow.

Narmu gathered his wits and the treasured hardwood shaft and made his way back to the desert camp. He searched the ground on the way for the right stone to be placed at the end of his prize to complete the spear. "My rage is what caused the accidental fall from the tree", he thought to himself. "I shall control my anger until I am face to face with this animal that I despise so. It will be a quick death for it and my revenge will be complete. I have killed it twice in my dreams already, I know what to expect".

There were many stones that were rejected along the way until a shiny triangular one caught his eye that would serve the purpose. It had a sharp tip with jagged edges. All he would need to do would be to cut a notch in the shaft where the stone would be inserted then lashed tightly with twine and covered with sap. He had fashioned the weapon in his mind and when he reached the camp, it was finished before sunset. He was ready for the night monster.

Narmu slept for a few hours until a half-moon was high. He made his way alone into the forest unafraid and full of hate. He was gone the rest of the night and at sunrise he returned to camp and tossed two large black ears at the feet of Helina. He was covered with blood from head to toe but had sustained not a scratch. Narmu collapsed on a grass mat in the middle of camp where he slept the entire day as the children cleaned and groomed him. His revenge was complete, and the killer was dead.

Chapter 27

The Descent

The charm and innocence of Peek had reminded the women from West, what they no longer were. Their ascension from darkness into the light of reason and compassion had been a painful rebirth through fire and death. The child's voice was a message from the heart, which stripped bare the eyes and ears to reveal truth and love where the light of forgiveness became the beacon that would guide them into a new land of compromise and hope. They would not go into that place with doubt and hatred, but would use a combination of thought and kindness to subdue the ignorant, and to carve out a niche for themselves. There was great optimism amidst the grief for Kick, and a consensus that she did not die in vain. They would proceed with caution.

The group worked together to form a defense in the form of an arsenal of new weapons, arrows with tips of stone. The bottom of the river was a bed of gravel from which the sharp and pointed tips were found. Several of the youngest dove repeatedly to retrieve them while others gathered the straight shafts of wood and sap from trees, while still others made the twine from the berry vines by stripping the fine bark and chewing it to the right texture for twisting around the arrows to attach the bits of stone. The sap was used to seal the twine and to affix a fin made from dry leaves to the bottom for stability. They were lined up to dry in the warm sun on a large flat rock in the middle of the clearing and by day's end there were hundreds. The girls were talking and singing all the while and at times a burst of laughter or giggling would erupt spontaneously through the entire clan. They discovered that work could be an agent of healing from grief. Panther was amazed at the phenomenon and would never forget it. The loss of a sister had always garnered feelings of revenge and hatred followed by deep sorrow. She found it interesting how being productive could be a diversion from the negative feelings that seemed so natural to her before. Being close to her sisters and working as one for a common cause gave meaning to her life for a time. The group was growing ever closer and each was becoming a little wiser.

As nighttime approached they decided to build a fire and have a big meal of muscles that were found while digging for stones in the river. They sat in a great circle and told stories from the past of their own experiences from before they came together as a group. The night was filled with tales of abandon and rape as pain escaped from them and went up into the sky like smoke from the fire as each girl told the most frightening or horrible event from their past. Tears were shed and laughter was sporadic as they could all identify with even the most wretched of experiences. Everyone retired in a circle of sleep around the fire with only two guards posted up the trail. Panther and Shasta sat by the river discussing their future.

"How could you even mention men Panther? Your words caused us great pain from memories we would rather forget". Panther did not speak for some time but tossed small pebbles into the river to see the current pull them along as they sank out of the moon's light to the bottom. Finally she spoke after much thought. "I am trying to make sense of this tragic world into which we are born Shasta. I feel like these pebbles that are pulled along by the current as they sink into darkness. I do not know why I am here or who, if anyone has put me here. You must admit that we have lost all faith in the invisible one who dwells in the desert. Even if he does exist, I hate him for the haunted world he has created. If he is not real, I hate myself for being a part of a people such as ours." "We have changed, you said it yourself", replied Shasta. "Have we? Our arrows are ready for war as we speak. Sometimes I think that it would be better to just die instead of playing this murderous game of life. How do these events happen, where two groups come together for the purpose of killing each other?" "I do not have your answer. I only know that if we don't protect ourselves we will die". "It's always that way," snapped Panther. "Why must it be so? I am certain that the people of that valley feel the same as we do. They must now be preparing to kill us to protect themselves". "Maybe they kill for pleasure, as we once did. They may be an evil people like ours from West, who relish in the pain and blood of others". Shasta was not angry but spoke as if she were searching for answers. " I don't know the answers to our problems in this life", Panther said softly. "I feel in my heart that there must be something else to this life than constant struggling and conflict. It makes no sense to me how the world can be so terrible yet so lovely. One day we have peace and feelings of love, while the next is full of war and hatred. One day the sky is blue and the air is sweet with flowers, while the next our world is afire". "Yes", agreed Shasta, and nothing more was said that night.

The morning was cool and misty with a thick fog hugging the ground. The fire had gone out and everyone had a chill but there was much energy and optimism in the group. Panther had decided to ask for volunteers to accompany her on the trip down the steep trail and made it clear to Peek that she must remain behind. Shasta would remain as well and assume leadership of the girls for if anything happened to the scouting party, Panther knew that she would make a good replacement for her. The twins, Santue and Free were willing and both were excellent with the bow. They were not tall but strong and agile. They wore their red hair tied back in a braid and no one could tell which one was which, so they talked to them as one since they were always together anyway. They could read each other's minds and Panther thought that they were really one person with two bodies.

Everyone helped them to prepare for their journey down into the valley of the unknown. Panther did not want to appear warlike, thus her reasoning for such a limited size expedition. They only took seven arrows each that the girls wrapped in bundles of long grass that they could attach to their waists with twine. The arrows were hidden yet easily accessible if needed, and the bundles had the appearance of bedding for sleep. Short bows were fashioned from strong willows that were slung over their bodies in a low profile so that they did not rise above the head. From a distance they would have the outward show of being unarmed and Panther hoped that they would not be perceived as a threat. They would carry no food or water for they were in a land of great abundance. The three red haired girls left camp followed by all who quietly wished them luck and touched them in a show of affection as they entered the fog shrouded trail. Shasta thought of the pebbles in the stream from the night before, disappearing into the dark current as Panther slid into the fog and out of sight. The women from West built a small fire and sat on the damp ground in a circle holding hands with their eyes closed for a long time without speaking. They were full of hope and at the same time fearful that the girls may not come back. Nothing was said and at mid day when the sun began to burn away the fog, they went about the routine of harvesting food and cleaning the campsite.

Panther led the way in silence through the fog with the twins right behind her. They would stop from time to time to listen for a rustling of weeds or a cracking twig, but the sound of the waterfall made it impossible to make out any faint noises. She thought that this was the most dangerous part of the descent for they were deaf. When they reached the body of Kick, Panther instructed Santue and Free to ready their bows while she hid the corpse in a deep thicket beside the trail. They stayed low to the ground and the tall grass concealed their activities. A marker in the form of a white stone was placed in the narrow trail so that even if they did not return to camp, the group would at least recover Kick for burial.

When they reached the edge of the precipice where the river dropped to the valley below, the fog lifted with the late morning sun's heat to reveal the lush and green landscape spreading out to the southern horizon. Steep purple mountains to the east and west hedged the valley while the ribbon of blue water snaked its way along the wide tropical forested flatland until it disappeared into a thin line that divided the valley in half. There was no sign of life except for large white birds that were pulling fish from the waterfall in mid flight. The pungent smell of orchids permeated the air to the point of intoxication and the women felt as though they were dreaming.

Panther led the way down the steep and winding trail that doubled back on itself again and again but the downhill travel was easy and beautiful. At the base of the waterfall there were enormous boulders piled up that turned the falling river into a fine mist before it settled into pools that emptied small streams into a larger pool which was where the river reassembled itself to continue its gentle journey through the valley. They never let their guard down in the midst of the tranquility, and decided to rest in a hidden clearing to the east of the river's bank. There they gathered some unknown fruit to eat that was sweet and luscious until they had their fill and were replenished enough to continue.

The group continued along the trail that followed the bank, for Panther decided to take the chance and seek out the people whom occupied this paradise, rather than covertly spying. She knew that she was taking a big chance but she thought hard about her conversation with Shasta about changing, and so decided to do her best to avoid bloodshed, even if it meant her own life. She told the twins to disarm, and the three stashed their weapons in a cache behind some large rocks. She wanted to gain the trust of the locals but if they were fired upon, they could run for the cache to make a stand behind the shelter of the rocks. They were all exceptional runners and she told the girls that if one took an arrow, the other two would retreat to the place of the weapons and make a stand to the death, or try to escape back up the trail to the campsite. If that happened, she told them to lead the group back through the cave and to never return to this valley.

Not long after they stashed the bows and arrows, a group of large hairy men rushed towards them from all directions. They were surrounded.

Chapter 28

Impetus

The conquering of the night beast was a great victory for the Helinites. The queen bent over and picked up the enormous black ears of the dead bear and held them to her breasts. It was she who was the nurturer of the great hunter Narmu. It was his passion for her that drove him to risk his life in the dark. These were her thoughts as he lay asleep, exhausted from his fight, but as he dreamed, his thoughts were on Jem, and all of the other children. He was their protector and provider. He would have died for any of them; in fact he nearly died for the dead child. His love was boundless and his own life meant nothing. Helina's fantasy as a goddess was growing but she would keep that to herself, along with her emergent obsession with the macabre.

Narmu awoke to laughter and the noise of a busy people making ready to enter the forest. He was surprised to see the children constructing stone tipped spears. There was a pile of pointed stones next to a stack of sticks where some of the children were busy tying the two together to fashion the weapons. It was quite organized were everyone participated, some gathering the materials while others prepared the twine or notched the ends of the wooden sticks. There was a finished pile of formidable halberds at the end of the assembly line. Helina called out," Take up your weapons. Today we drive into the new land, which we will claim as our own. Nothing can stop us for we have the father sun as our master. We are his children whom he favors above all other creatures!" Narmu stood to his feet to see the young warriors grabbing the spears and lining up like soldiers going into battle. Helina walked over to him and took his hand while passing him his own weapon that he'd worked so hard to build. She had tied the bear's ears to it along with a single hawk's feather like the ones she wore for her crown. He held it tight as she kissed his cheek and thanked him. He remembered the dream of her killing the bear while he was knocked out beneath the burnt hardwood tree, and he remembered that her hair had been red. It was her face in the dream but her anger was from someone else, never before seen in anyone that he had ever known. He thought of her licking Tep's blood from his hands and her story in the desert of her being a goddess. When he had killed the black beast of the night, he was full of the rage that the red haired Helina had in his dream. The thought of this rage made his skin crawl and the hair stood up on the back of his neck. He jerked his hand from Helina out of repulsion, which startled her momentarily. He then smiled and returned the kiss on her cheek. "Yes!" he said. "Today we move into the forest in search of what is ours." Helina grinned, exposing her white teeth, something she had not done since she was a child. "Children", began her oration. "We are the masters of wherever we go, but our gods dictate our path. Our temple to the sun in the woods is a sacred place, for it is the heart of our religion and it will always be the place of our beginning as a powerful people. We shall build a new temple to him when we reach our new home, and to the moon and hawk as well. Let us all close our eyes now in silence, with our faces toward the father, to feel his life giving warmth and to know his guiding spirit". Everyone did as she commanded without hesitations accept Jason. He looked at the queen in her trance and worried about the children's future. He noticed that none of the young lovers had their eyes open and that the children were lined up in perfect order of obedience and reverence. It frightened him to see that their individuality had vanished and that they were more of a collective than ever. They were controlled by the queen and would die for her. The new religion had come to dominate their souls and he thought that Helina was using it for that purpose. Jason looked over his right shoulder and his eyes caught Narmu's. They were the only ones in the group with open eyes and they stared at each other for the rest of the ceremony. Narmu's gaze was one without perceptible emotion but they both knew that they were of one mind.

The group was anxious to get started on their new adventure but Narmu was ever vigilant of recklessness and oversight. His main concern was the safety of the children so he thought that the orderliness of an army was a good idea for now. He would take the lead on their penetration into the forest while Jason took the rear. The queen was in the middle and surrounded by four hunters with their spears. Everyone was armed and would be watchful of danger or movement in the brush. They started at a brisk walk while leaving the desert and when they approached the edge of the forest they became more attentive to their environment. The thought of the bear was foremost in their minds but they had a new sense of security with the new weapons and the watchful eye of the sun. Although the children trusted and loved their queen, they were more at ease when Narmu was around. They could sense that he would fight for them and Helina was aware of this. She felt that it was good for the group to feel secure but she was also troubled that Narmu could one day become a threat to her authority. That was not of great concern to her now for she felt that his needed strength outweighed the possibility of him being potential competition, and besides, he was loyal to her as far as she could tell and in her mind she thought that he probably loved her.

Jason was also comforting for the children in a different way. His weapon in protecting them was his words, and they had seen the power of his persuasion when they needed someone to speak for them, but it would be Narmu who would have the final say concerning their safety from not only the monsters of the night, but also from the wrath of the queen as well. The children had two great allies, one who would speak for them with intellect and the other who would kill for them with his brute strength and cunning. They were both motivated by their compassion for the innocent. Helina was aware of the complicated dynamics within her new government and she was always thinking of ways to preserve her power, above even the welfare of the group. She was aware of the potential for a coup in an extreme situation, as Jason's influence had grown substantially since the stoning, not only with the group but with Narmu also. For the first time, she was considering Jason to be a problem and was now plotting to herself what could be done about him. She would wait concerning this as it had not yet become a problem, and besides, she had plenty on her mind now with the trek into the forest.

The green of the lush and moist forest was refreshing to the eyes, and the sound of birds was like music to the heart. Life. The desert was so barren and quiet, and Helina had come to love its openness and warm winds at night. She loved the stars in their clarity with the dry air, and how the sand dunes sparkled in the moonlight. The forest, although lovely and living, was full of mystery and darkness, which she found disturbing. In the desert she felt powerful, as she could see all around, but the darkened woods filled her with anxiety at the thought of the unknown. The bear was merely an omen of things to come, she thought. Where there is life, there is danger. She knew how to confront the dangers of the desert. Thirst, hunger and heat were now simple puzzles, but the wild animal was unpredictable, like the dogs of the woods. Her vision was diminished in the tree-darkened meadows and the walls and ceiling of green were claustrophobic. She could not bear not knowing what lay ahead. The desert let her mind drift and to consider options but the new landscape she was now in confined her thoughts to the moment, the present. There was no room to anticipate, or time to contemplate the sister moon or the hawk.

Helina did not let her anxiety show as they pushed further into the darkness. The blue sky was now gone and she looked over her shoulder to see the last glimpse of yellow sand disappear and turn to green. The children could hardly contain their excitement as they pushed ahead, wanting to see what was beyond the next grove of trees. The smell of pine was thick and an occasional hare or deer darted away into the brush. The woods soon became so thick that a trail had to be cleared ahead which slowed their progress substantially. At times they had to circumvent entire groves that took them either to the north or the south as a detour. They would maintain a general westward course though and by nightfall the land began to rise, making the journey more difficult. Narmu told everyone that it would be uphill for several days and that is when Helina called out to make camp for the night.

A fire was built by a large boulder, in a clearing near a small stream. Some boys made quick work of killing several hare and a small deer for dinner and the smell of cooking meat permeated the campsite by dark. Everyone was enjoying the meal while Helina took her spear and went into the dark woods alone. Narmu was concerned and followed her meandering walk when he finally caught up with her to ask where she was going. "I hate the forest", she said abruptly. "I am trying to consult my sister moon but I cannot even see her face. Her light filters down to me through these large trees but I must see her to know her will and to seek her advice." Narmu laughed and replied, "What advice do you require on this lovely night in this enchanted place". "It's not enchanted. It is dark and full of mystery. I loathe the smell of pine and the stars do not shine. I could not see the hawk either if he were to fly right over my head". "If I were the sister moon, Helina, I would tell you to forget about advice this night and to enjoy the company of your loved ones." Narmu took her in his arms. "And if I were the hawk, I would tell you that your love surrounds you but you do not see it. I would think that the moon and the hawk are busy on this night and that you should seek your answers in your own heart, and in your lover's arms". Narmu pulled Helina's hair back and kissed her. She embraced him and kissed him back as the lovers fell softly to the leave covered ground and for a time, she thought only of Narmu.

Helina awoke before morning with moonlight on her face. She saw her sister through a small opening in the canopy of the dense forest, as Narmu was still asleep. She pondered the moon as it passed slowly by the opening, and hoped she would speak during that fleeting visit. She felt nothing from her nor heard her voice in her head as she listened patiently. Despair washed over her like an ocean wave as the moon slid out of site and Helina was convinced that the gods were not happy. She got up quietly and walked back to camp leaving Narmu asleep alone. There she sat by the burnt out embers of the fire and contemplated her next move. She was certain now that her relationship with Narmu was wrong or surely the moon would have spoken to her. She never heard the hawk cry that night and she thought about Mik. Never had she been so confused but one thing that she did know was that she had to take control over the group once more in its entirety. She would not need a counsel such as Jason or a consort such as Narmu. She would need to reassert herself as the sole ruler and the goddess of her people. The moon and the hawk's voice were clear to her in their silence.

The morning was full of the sounds of laughter and children playing. Narmu strolled back to camp alone to see the rowdiness and running of the group and just in time to witness Helina explode into a disturbing outburst of admonishment, commanding the children to break camp and to stop their childish behavior. He said nothing but joined in to ready the group for the next day of travel. Jason was helping to tie Caron and Geenah to their stretchers, as they were still unable to walk from the stoning. Everyone obeyed the queen without question and Narmu could not catch a glance from her for she avoided looking at him or Jason. He felt foolish and angry at her sudden behavior but it did not surprise him. He made up his mind to never sleep with her or kiss her again.

Helina pressed the group hard into the forest and was

determined to make it to the foothills of the mountains before dark. The travel became difficult after they crossed over a low ridge to discover a large expanse of a dried swamp that clearly had to be traversed. There was nothing but tall dried reeds so thick that walking was made impossible. Narmu built a device made from woven pine limbs that was a rectangle which was used to flatten the reeds as they pushed down on it with mere body weight, thus making a perfect trail of flattened reeds to walk on. It was wide enough to walk two men across and the queen was thrilled at their progress. The children were delighted with the trail and took great joy in the making of the road. Helina grew annoyed at their laughter but kept quiet. She was happy to see the sun in its full glory looking up from the reeds but when the afternoon arrived the sun could no longer be seen and the shadows depressed her.

Jason came running up from the rear and approached the queen. "Geenah is very ill from her wounds and cannot travel"! "Impossible", she replied quickly. "But why? What's the hurry to arrive someplace where we've never been? She has a fever and I fear that she is near death". "Then what difference does it make? When her fire burns out, she will die. That is the will of the father." Her words were the final say as she gestured with her hand to stop the conversation. He grunted with angst as he ran back to the sick one. Narmu was unaware of the occurrence as he led the road making in the front with the children laughing. Geenah fell unconscious and started convulsing while Caron held her hand from his stretcher. The rear of the line came to a stop to let the drama of death unfold without the distraction of movement as the rest of the group pushed ahead. Jason decided to disobey Helina out of respect for the dying and the grieving. Caron was crying as his lover died while those at hand consoled him. It was a touching moment that should have gained more respect from the queen and those who witnessed the event would not forget it and they would not forgive her. Her body was wrapped in a blanket of dried grass and Jason said some words in her memory. They carried her body with them and did not rush to join the others, as the trail was the only way to go anyway.

The Helinites came out of the dried swamp and arrived at the base of the foothills as the sun was setting. Narmu commanded his hunters to search the nearby woods for any danger and to hunt for food while the others established a campsite. When everyone had come out of the reeds it was noticed that Jason and the sick children were missing, along with six others. Narmu went back alone to find them and he did so in a short time. "Why didn't you inform us that Geenah had died"? He asked of Jason. "I beseeched the queen to rest and told her that the girl could not travel but her response was one of disdain. We stayed behind to let her die in dignity, not wanting to add the movement of travel to her pain." Narmu put his arm around Jason and the two men held back their tears for the sake of the others. "She shall have a proper burial and I shall confront Helina on this matter at the proper time. Come my friend, let us tell the others." Narmu's words comforted Jason but he knew that the queen's heart was growing cold and that her appetite for power was her new preoccupation.

The hunters returned with deer and some nuts and a fire had been built in the center of a large clearing with a ring of large stones around it. The body of Geenah lay on a stand made from tree limbs and she was still bound to the stretcher, wrapped in the grass blanket. Everyone gathered around and sat quietly as the queen was about to speak. They were expecting words about how kind Geenah had been or what a sweet wit she had possessed, but Helina began her oration in a manner never seen. "The father had condemned this child to death for her sin. We denied his authority by showing mercy when mercy was not ours to give". She stood on a large rock by the fire with her arms raised and spoke admonishingly with a loud voice of anger. "Jem paid with his life for our transgression. The sun sent the night monster to devour our poor little innocent Jem. Now he has claimed what was due to him, and that is the life of Geenah, a sinner! She will not receive last rights from us for she forfeited those rights when she broke the law of god. Her body must be burned in this fire to rid us of her mistake." She pointed to two hunters and then to the fire. " Place her on the flames. Her fire went out long ago during the stoning. It is the will of the father". The two hunters placed her body in the fire and she burned up quickly with the grass blanket as kindling. Many girls began to sob and the queen told them that crying for the damned was a sin as well and they hushed themselves straight away.

"Caron!" Helina pointed her accusing finger at the outstretched boy. "Now you must die. Place him in the fire now before the night monster comes to devour us all"! "No"! Yelled Narmu. "You hold your tongue. You are the cause of this injustice. You are a murderer and a blasphemer. These children should have died a quick death long ago but you intervened and killed Tep, the keeper of the law. These children have suffered long and Jem has paid with his life."

Helina had worked the group into frenzy as the smell of Geenah's burning corpse filled the air. They grabbed up the stretcher of Caron and tossed him into the flames as Narmu lunged forward. A hundred children grabbed he and Jason as Caron's screams suddenly ceased. Everyone stopped to watch the fire for several moments until the crackling flames subsided when one of Tep's soldiers yelled out, "Justice is served"! Followed by a collective cry from the Helinites, "Justice is served"!

Narmu and Jason left the camp immediately and retreated to the dark forest for the rest of the night.

Chapter 29

Captivity

Panther and the twins were so startled by the site of the brutes that defending themselves never occurred to them. Half animal looking people surrounded them with large spears, bows and arrows. Their faces were huge with large jaws and protruding eyes. It was obvious that they were males beneath their hairy bodies for they wore no clothing but belts of rope for carrying arrows and stone knives. They were not tall but were stocky with short legs and bare feet that were covered with hair except for the toes, which had the appearance of leather. No one spoke and the girls did not move for fear of being shot by the dozens of stone tipped arrows that were pointing at them at close range. The men were wide-eyed and nervous and seemed as startled as their prisoners. The waterfall was the only sound for the longest time until one of the archers grunted a noise when the girls were grabbed from all directions, wrestled to the ground and tied like animals with bound feet and hands. Panther was looking up at the sky when everything went black. Consciousness came slowly with feeling in her feet first, and then a terrible pain on the top of her head. She tried to touch it but discovered that her hands were still tied. There was no light or sounds but then a tiny flame sparked in the distance and there were the sounds of crickets. The air was cool on her body from all sides and she knew that she was in the open. An effort to call out to Free and Santue was useless. Her voice would not function. She could not raise her head and cold fluid ran into her ear that was blood. Daylight revealed the depth of her dilemma. She was in a cage made of sticks and rope suspended high above the ground in a tree. There was no sign of the twins but her view was blocked for the most part by the broad leaves of the treetops. She could see straight down through the bars of wood to the ground, which was a great distance. Her head was spinning from being knocked out and she found the gash on her head that was already healing. Her clothing and hair was soaked with dried blood and there was pain in her chest from broken ribs. Someone had removed the ropes from her hands, which she didn't remember. She lost consciousness once more. "Why am I in this tree? I have seen no one since being captured. Where are the twins?" Panther was talking to herself aloud still suspended in the cage. "I am thirsty". Her voice retreated to thoughts. I hear the sound of men grunting. They are so strange looking, like half beasts. They are coming toward my tree. They are lowering me down to the ground by ropes. They are so strong. Be calm Panther and do not show fear. Why are they staring at me? Don't touch me you monster or I'll claw your bug eyes out by the roots. I don't understand them. Their words are just grunting. "I'm thirsty"! You idiot. A female! She is bringing me water. And fruit! Eat it. You will need all the strength you can get. Oh no, up again! "Where are the other girls"! They're laughing at me. We'll see who laughs, you apes. Up in the tree again. Well, how long can this stupid game go on? Where are they going? What are they? You have to get out of this tree. I can't stay up here forever; there must be a way out of this cage. I'll try to break the bars. This is stout wood; I'll try the ropes. This could take awhile. Why would they bring a female to feed me? I wish they would at least let me communicate with them. I need a stone to cut with; I'll try my teeth. This isn't working. I wonder where the twins are. Oh, my ribs hurt. Day after day it's the same thing. Once a day they lower the cage to laugh at me and then that female brings me water and fruit. How long have I been here? I need to get out of here. I cannot stand up and the bars are hard to sleep on. I wonder what the girls in camp are doing? I hope they obey me and retreat to the cave and beyond to the path.

I must try something today. I think that they are amused by me, like a pet or something. Here we go, this time I'll make a change happen, for better or worse. Something must change here. Have your laughs you monkeys. Here she comes. Water. Now the fruit, I have you bitch.

I'll bite your hand off! "Let me out of here"! …. Darkness.

Now what? It is so dark. I'm no longer in the trees. It smells like dirt. Oh no I'm underground. This is definitely different, a turn for the worse I'm afraid.

Five days pass before Panther hears a sound in her grave.

They left her with water to drink and nothing else. She was ten feet under the earth in the same cage with no way out. No light or food. The air was stale. She heard digging above and then a shaft of light beamed down on her face. "Let me out of here"! Her captors threw water and fruit down into the cage then slammed the lid back onto the tomb.

I cannot take this any longer. I want to die. I feel like I'm in a void suspended in space with no time. No sun. No people to talk with. I miss my sisters so. I must stop thinking completely or surely I'll go mad.

Panther had no idea how long she had been underground; it could have been days or months. She had stopped thinking at all and only responded when food was thrown down into the pit just before starvation set in. The lid to her grave opened up wide and filled the hole with a light so brilliant that she was blinded. She felt the cage rise up slowly and settle on the ground gently. Her captors tied her hands and blindfolded her. Two of the men carried her for a long time for she was unable to walk. Then she heard the sound of the waterfall in the distance and it got louder with every step that they took. For the first time since her capture she had hope, and for the first time since she stopped thinking, she wanted to live.

She was laid on the ground by the large pond beneath the waterfall and her hands were untied. It was a struggle for her to remove the blindfold but when she finally did there was no one around. She was alone and free.

Panther was much too weak to attempt the climb up the trail to the others but she didn't have to wait long for help. Shasta lifted her up under her arms and tossed her emaciated body over her shoulder and ran up the trail until they reached the precipice. "Shasta my dear girl. You have disobeyed my orders". She whispered. "You are in no condition to give orders sister. Save your strength and don't talk". A dozen other sisters were waiting at the top and they all touched her in affection as they made their way back to camp. Panther rested for several days and was hand fed until she regained the strength to eat on her own.

"Have you seen the twins"? She asked. "No. They are missing. We were about to give up on you". Shasta's reply was heartbreaking for Panther for she was fond of the girls. "How long"? "Two full moons". Shasta said quietly. "Now rest some more and try not to think". Panther laughed for a long time at the absurdity of the statement. Shasta looked puzzled as she pulled a blanket over her and she laughed herself to sleep.

Lightning Source UK Ltd.
Milton Keynes UK
UKHW011959270519
343419UK00002B/16/P